PRAISE FOR
GRAVE INTERVENTION

· · ✦ · ✦ · ·

"Shira Shiloah creates a masterful story of intrigue ... *GRAVE INTERVENTION* will appeal to thriller and mystery audiences, as well as those who appreciate a solid story filled with satisfyingly unpredictable twists and turns throughout."

—*Midwest Book Review*

"Real life stressors collide with mysterious hauntings in Shira Shiloah's newest thriller, *GRAVE INTERVENTION*. A beautifully drawn family drama that encompasses fascinating history and realistic medical scenes, Shiloah presents a unique and compelling story of life, love and the power of forgiveness."

—*Tammy Euliano, MD*
Author of Fatal Intent and Misfire

"Readers of paranormal fiction and suspense thrillers will find themselves engrossed in this finely paced, sinister tale of a family haunted by the spirit of a historical figure."

–*Kirkus*

"Like Micheal Crichton and Robin Cook, Dr. Shiloah has employed medical expertise to craft an engaging and harrowing tale that's as real as it is imaginative. If only nine out of ten doctors endorsed this novel it is because the tenth died from fright."

–*T.J. Tranchell, Author of Cry Down Dark and Tell No Man*

Notable Winner, 2022 Gutsy Great Novelist Chapter One Prize.

—*Selected by Joan Dempsey*

·· ◆ ◆ ◆ ··

ALSO BY SHIRA SHILOAH

EMERGENCE

·· ◆ ◆ ◆ ··

GRAVE
INTERVENTION

SHIRA SHILOAH

SALTY AIR
PUBLISHING

HARDBACK ISBN: 978-1-7351930-6-9
EBOOK ISBN: 978-1-7351930-7-6
PAPERBACK ISBN: 978-1-7351930-9-0
AUDIOBOOK ISBN: 978-1-7351930-5-2

Names: Shiloah, Shira, author.

Title: Grave intervention / Shira Shiloah.

Description: [Memphis, Tennessee] : [Salty Air Publishing], [2022]

Identifiers: ISBN: 978-1-7351930-6-9 (hardback) | 978-1-7351930-9-0 (paperback) | 978-1-7351930-7-6 (ebook) | 978-1-73519-305-2 (audiobook)

Subjects: LCSH: Physicians--Illinois--Naperville--Fiction. | Spirits--Fiction. | Dead--Fiction. | Suburban life--Fiction. | Naperville (Ill.)--Fiction. | LCGFT: Ghost stories. | Paranormal fiction. | Thrillers (Fiction) | Medical fiction. | BISAC: FICTION / Thrillers / Historical. | FICTION / Thrillers / Suspense. | FICTION / Ghost.

Classification: LCC: PS3619.H547 G73 2022 | DDC: 813/.6--dc23

Cover Design by James T. Egan
Book Interior and E-book Design by Amit Dey

This is dedicated to courageous immigrants,
especially my Syrian-Yemenite mother, Frida Medini
and my Iraqi father, Dr. Jacob Shiloah.

"To be dead is to be prey for the living."

Jean-Paul Sartre

CHAPTER ONE

Naperville, Illinois
December 13, 2018

*A*mir bounded up the wooden stairwell to Sami's room and found her and Camille asleep. Though he was running late for his first case, he took a moment to study them from the door; the light from the hallway illuminated the darkened bedroom. Camille's arm was draped over their daughter, and their breathing was synchronized. He wondered what time she'd left their room to cuddle Sami in her "big girl bed," a present his parents shipped last week. The crib remained in the corner of the room. He knew disassembling it would be another bittersweet milestone for Camille and didn't want to rush her.

"My sleeping beauties," Amir said, as he stroked his wife's sandy blonde hair out of her eyes. He kissed her forehead. "Babe, it's already seven."

Camille didn't stir, so he turned on the bedside lamp. She rubbed her eyes and squinted.

"I have a first case start," Amir said. "You getting up?"

"*Des bisous,*" she murmured, asking for a kiss, and pulling him to her pillow.

He nuzzled her slender neck, inhaling the scent of her, then reached over to kiss their daughter's head, full of hair as black as his, only baby-fine. "I'm hopping in the shower. *Yallah,* time to get up, love."

There was no light coming from the master bathroom skylight, and in an hour, the black sky would turn gray in the heart of Chicago's winter. As the water streamed onto Amir's face, he was startled by a sound. He turned his head to the right. It was a voice. A male voice. He looked through the foggy glass door at the vacant bathroom.

He was motionless as his naturally slow heart rate surged. A man was speaking, the words muffled as if something was covering his mouth.

I can't rest.

He cut off the water and listened with intent, but except for the sound of the furnace pumping heat through the ducts, the house was silent. He stepped out of the shower, grabbed a towel off the rack, and went to the kitchen. He confirmed the house alarm was on and bolted upstairs to find his girls both still asleep.

He looked out the window and studied the backyard. He could see his grandmother's apartment on Sunrise's top floor, the assisted living community she lived in across the way. Her lights were off. The Naperville Fire Department, next door to her, was dark as well. He peered out the front window from the landing and viewed the cove. Christmas lights flickered in the neighborhood, but there were none in his yard. He recognized his neighbor by his gait, bundled in a ski jacket and earmuffs, his unleashed terrier in front of him. It was probably "Limping Liam" calling out after the dog; his imagination had conjured up crazy sounds.

He looked again in Sami's bedroom and quietly shut the door, convinced there was no intruder. He wouldn't wake Camille again. Another day at home wouldn't hurt.

···❖❖❖···

Amir preferred to jog the route to the hospital, cutting through North Central College and onto the path along the DuPage River, but not when the ground was thick with snow and ice. And not when he was late. He drove past the hospital's "Wings of Hope Angel Garden" and turned into the physician parking garage. He waved to Jade as she got out of her Camry.

"You're running late, too, Dr. Price," Amir said as they walked through the sliding glass doors together. "Hopefully, no one will notice us."

"Around here, they wiretap," she laughed, referring to the hospital's scandalous past when their CEO worked with the FBI on an extortion case against the governor. "I'm certain we're on video as we speak. You, me, and my Afro." She patted the thick curls on her head.

"That sounds like a song." Amir pushed the elevator button up.

"Miss Dee will see if we get off the elevator now," she said and tugged at his winter coat sleeve. "Let's take the stairs, future Chairman."

They climbed the three flights, and Jade scanned her badge to enter the radiology suite. She waved goodbye and went into the ladies' locker room. Amir hung his coat on a hook in the empty doctor's lounge and went to interventional radiology's pre-operative holding.

"Look what drifted in," Lexi said. "It's Naperville's hottest M.D."

Dubbed "Sexy Lexi" by his male cohorts, Lexi, an interventional radiology nurse with a pin-up girl figure, was new to the hospital. Her scrubs were not the standard hospital issue. She bought the high-end kind, slim fit with multiple pockets, and tailored them to fit her ample backside. Today, in bright pink, she walked toward him. "Your patient's ready, Dr. Hadad. And your pre-med student's changing into scrubs."

Amir, with his olive skin, slender yet muscular frame, and long lashes framing his light brown eyes, was well accustomed to female attention. Now that he was married, he'd learned to dodge suggestive curveballs and lived by his father's motto, "Keep your hands in your pockets." He pulled the floppy hair off his forehead and tucked it into a surgical cap before greeting his patient, Mrs. Amber Trim. Seated next to her stretcher was Mr. Trim, who was anything but.

"Any questions about the procedure?" Amir smiled and rested his hands on the stretcher's railing.

"How long will she hurt afterwards?" the husband said, clutching his wife's purse on his lap.

"Usually, some ibuprofen and one or two Percocet are all you need for the uterine cramping."

Mrs. Trim, with a petite hand, patted Amir's firm one. "You do whatever it takes to stop the bleeding. I can handle a little pain, but I can't take another month of soaked pads."

"Let's head to the procedure room," he said and motioned to Lexi. "We'll give you some relaxation medicine."

As Lexi wheeled the stretcher into the suite, Amir went to the control room and pulled up MRI images. He'd studied them last night on his home station, and confirmed his approach now. His patient had one transmural fibroid causing her dysfunctional uterine bleeding. He looked into the suite, through the control room's leaded glass wall that allowed a view, and saw the patient lying on the imaging table. Mrs. Hunter prepped her right groin with chlorhexidine. Lexi, at the head of the table, crouched to avoid the ceiling-mounted imaging arm.

Amir pressed the speaker button and leaned closer to the microphone. "Lexi, please give two and two. I'll go scrub."

He put on the lead apron with his name embroidered on the front, securing the Velcro across his waist. As he was looking for his thyroid shield, the student from North Central entered the room wearing it around his neck. "Welcome," Amir said as he found one in the anesthesia department's stash.

"I'm Boaz." The eager student reminded Amir of himself at that age.

"Boaz, that," he said, pointing to the fibroid on the MRI image, "is today's enemy. The uterine artery that feeds this fibroid will be my target. Once I embolize it, the fibroid starves, shrinks, and dies. Her uterus will slough off the invader and be healthy again." An image of Camille in the ICU, hysterical and crying, came to him.

"You can scrub and stand next to me," Amir said. "Just don't touch anything or Mrs. Hunter will bark at us."

· · ✦ ✦ ✦ ✦ · ·

When the procedure was underway, the patient under sterile blue drapes, and her right groin exposed, Amir threaded a metal guidewire into her femoral artery. Using the fluoroscopy imaging, he snaked it further into the uterine artery. As he placed the catheter, he heard a whisper.

Jaysus. Ever kill a man?

"Excuse me?" Amir looked at Boaz.

"The plastic you'll inject inside the artery, is that permanent?"

Amir pivoted, squinting to see inside the control room. "Is someone in there?"

"No," Lexi said, still at the head of the bed. Mrs. Trim was snoring. "Why?"

Amir looked again at Boaz; did he think this was some joke? This patient's life was in his hands, it wasn't a time for whispering crazy shit in his ear. "Go watch from the control room. You're distracting me."

Boaz's ears turned bright pink as he stepped away from the procedure table. "Yes sir, I didn't mean to interrupt." He walked out of the room.

"Lexi, her vitals okay?"

"One hundred percent on two-liter nasal cannula, and sleeping like a teenager. Are *you* okay?"

He watched the fluoroscopy monitor as he injected the vessel. He'd be sure to comment on Boaz's student evaluation form.

CHAPTER TWO

"Sami?" Camille, with her hand on the stair railing, called out. "Savtah is here." Camille cherished Savtah Sabiha, Amir's grandmother. Sabiha exemplified strength and resilience, everything Camille felt she didn't have.

Though she loved her, Camille disliked unannounced visits. Using her walker, Sabiha could step out of her place at Sunrise, shuffle across Chicago Avenue, open the backyard gate, and appear at Camille's doorstep. Snow and ice on the ground didn't deter her, but if it was raining, she'd order the building's shuttle to drop her off in front. Sometimes she'd even let herself in if Camille didn't answer the doorbell, which would set off the house alarm and trigger an alert call from the security system. The safety code word she gave to the dispatcher was now, "Sabiha."

Camille wished everyone close to her —Sabiha, her sister, and especially Amir, would stop hovering over her as if she were the fragile egg perched on a ledge in the nursery book. "All the king's horses and all the king's men could not put Humpty together again." She read aloud, in her bedtime routine for Sami, silently agreeing. Once broken, really, what was the point.

"Samira!" Camille's voice louder this time.

A patter of footsteps and then Sami, draped in a Disney *Frozen* nightgown, came down the stairs into the foyer. She ran into Sabiha's open arms.

"Savtah, play dress up."

Sabiha smoothed down Sami's unbrushed hair and kissed the top of her head. "*Yaldah metuka,* sweet girl. Why aren't you at kinder music playing with other children?" She glanced at Camille, who stood in the kitchen also still in a nightshirt, preparing a cappuccino in her espresso machine.

"Mommy sleep. Come…" She pulled Sabiha's arthritic hand toward her parents' bedroom. "Play."

"In a minute, *metuka*, go ahead." Sabiha took off her winter coat and draped it over her walker as Sami went to her mother's closets. "Camille, what's your plan for the day? I thought you were volunteering?"

"They do not need the help of a former actress," Camille said and handed her the cappuccino in a porcelain mug. "I stopped going." In truth, Camille was embarrassed for even offering to help the local high school drama department. No one had asked her; she just showed up and assumed her off-Broadway reputation would precede her. It had not. The drama teacher saw her as a wannabe or a has-been; Camille wasn't sure which. She left without mentioning her previous acting career, or her singing ability. "I have plenty to do, keeping up with Sami. I do not need to volunteer like some desperate housewife of a doctor."

"No one thinks that. You have so much talent."

Camille looked away. She wasn't going to argue with a widow. "Come. Humor the child, not me. Next year she will be in school and you will miss having her home."

···◆◆◆◆···

Camille sat at her vanity mirror as Sabiha dressed her daughter. Sami had plenty to try on, as Camille's wardrobe was extensive. New clothes arrived once a month from her mother in France, but most had the tags still attached. "Americans have no taste," Camille's mom, Renée, speaking only in French, regularly said on FaceTime calls, frustrated to see Camille in baggy sweatshirts and jeans. "You must not lose your French beauty, your style. Your husband's a dashing doctor, be proud of how you look together."

Camille made the mistake of telling her about the New Year's Eve Heroes of Healing Gala Amir wanted them to attend. Sami had put on the designer charmeuse dress Renée sent her for the affair. The long fabric gathered on the floor around Sami like a halo, and the straps held the fabric at her two-and-half-year-old child's belly. She looked so cute and tiny, and so pleased with herself. Camille smiled at her.

"I'm princess." Sami gathered some fabric in her hands.

"Such a beautiful dress." Sabiha touched the emerald silk against Sami's cheek. "Maybe we can see it on Mommy?"

Camille shot her a look.

"Mommy!" Sami wriggled out of the dress and offered it to her mother. "Mommy put on."

Camille bent to kiss her forehead as she took the dress. "Okay, but after this, we will go to the Children's Museum and paint." She stepped into the walk-in closet and shut the door. Pulling off her nightshirt, she quickly put on the dress and stepped back out. She looked in the mirror. A faint upturn of her lips formed. The dress draped gracefully on her slender shoulders, and the color accentuated her eyes. Even in no make-up, with her hair in a ponytail, she knew she was striking.

"Like a movie star… your Mommy looks like a star," Sabiha said.

"Mommy pretty." Sami touched her mother's scar through the fabric.

Camille recoiled.

CHAPTER THREE

⋅⋅◆◆◆⋅⋅

*A*mir stepped into the laundry room from the garage, stripped out of his scrubs, and dropped them in the washing machine. A rule Camille insisted on—no hospital germs in the house.

Wearing just his boxers, he entered the foyer. The home had an open layout, with the dining room spilling into the foyer and den on either side, creating one continuous space running east and west through the house. A swinging door at the south end of the dining room, propped permanently open for continuous access to the kitchen, was as inviting as the long-awaited Sami embrace after a workday.

He found Camille and Sami in the den watching *Mister Rogers' Neighborhood*. He'd grown up on the show, but his French wife was as naive to it as Sami.

"Daddy!" She ran to him, and he picked her up, swinging her before she wrapped her legs around him as he hugged her.

"Best part of my day," Amir said and kissed her cheeks. Twice on each side, a Sami rule ingrained by her Aunt Viva.

"I paint today." She pointed to her creation on the dining room table. Though the last night of Hanukkah was three days ago, the table still had their menorah and dreidels on it.

Amir carried her to the table and held up the painting of disorganized scribbles. "Such brilliant use of color."

Sami beamed.

Camille remained on the couch, her expression sad. He could tell she'd been crying and saw the episode "Death of a Goldfish" was streaming. He thought her grief would've let up by now; two-and-a-half years in, the depression showed no sign of leaving. He wished she'd see a therapist. He'd broach the topic again with Viva; maybe she'd listen to her sister.

"Let's get Mommy," he whispered into Sami's ear, and she squealed with delight. He put Sami on his shoulders and said, "One, two, three… attack the Mommy… here we come." He walked behind the couch and bent at his waist so both he and Sami could hug Camille. "Give Mommy kisses. So many kisses."

Camille reached for them, pulling them into an embrace with each arm, and taking Sami onto her lap. "Cuddle puddle," she said. She kissed them both. "How was your day?"

Yer lady's a grand feen.

The voice. He heard the words clearly. He surveyed the room and saw the front door was closed; no one was there but the three of them. He turned behind him and glanced at the hallway leading from the garage into the foyer.

"Did you hear that?" Amir whispered.

"Hear what? You're scaring me."

Jaysus, her legs. You lucky bastard.

"Take Sami now. Get in the car." He went to the kitchen, grabbed his phone and a carving knife from the drawer. "Go."

Camille gathered their coats from the laundry room, set Sami on the washing machine and put shoes on her. "Come with me, Sami. Daddy wants us to take a drive." Camille carried her and Sami dropped her doll while reaching for her father.

"Daddy, come."

"I'll be right there, baby. I have to get dressed. Go with Mommy." He watched from the garage entrance as Camille strapped Sami into her rear facing car seat in the back of the Tesla SUV. She held her palms up to him.

"Where am I going?"

"Go to Malnati's, order for us. I'll be right there." He closed the garage door after they drove away, and went inside. He walked from the kitchen to the den. Sami's toys and dolls were scattered on the carpet. Another episode of *Mister Rogers'* had started. He turned off the television. The room had turned colder. Amir checked the front windows, all were sealed. He shivered.

Yer lady's grand.

"Come out where I can see you, you psychopath. Who's there?" Amir dialed 911 on his phone. "Police. I have an intruder." He put on jeans and a sweater, grabbed his coat and wallet, and went out the front door holding the carving knife.

· · + ◆ + · ·

Amir paced at the end of the driveway watching his house. Everything looked in order. The contractor had replaced the storm-damaged wood siding along the front after he renovated their master bathroom. All the windows were closed and intact. A police car arrived; its lights flashed red but its siren was silent. He held his hands up, having left the knife inside the mailbox, as one of the male officers approached. Skinny and tall, with enormous hands, the officer reminded him of a patient with Marfan's syndrome. He read the name on the badge: *Nichols.*

"Are you the owner of the house?"

"Yes, Officer Nichols," he said. "My name's Dr. Amir Hadad. I have my ID in my pocket if you need it."

Nichols reached out his hand, examined the ID, and handed it back. "What's been going on, Dr. Hadad?"

"I was in the den and heard a man with an accent. But I didn't see him, I don't know where he's hiding. My wife and daughter were here but I sent them away. No one's in there but him."

The other officer approached while speaking into his walkie-talkie, "Backup requested. 937 Oak Branch."

"Did they hear him, see anything?" Nichols said. "Any sign of forced entry?"

"It's cold, as if he smashed a window. But I couldn't find which one."

"We're going to ask you to wait at the bottom of the cove for your safety. I don't want you in the line of fire, out here like a paper target."

Amir walked to the end of the cove and watched as two more police sedans arrived. A neighbor's driveway basketball hoop had ice on it. His phone vibrated with Camille's text alert.

> *Pizza arrived, is everything okay?*

> ...

> *Cops are checking the house, stay there. I'm safe, down the street watching.*

The crescent moon broke from the clouds, and he could see his breath in the air. The bitter December cold was expected to worsen over the next week. He watched as two officers entered the front door with their guns drawn, while the others surrounded the house. A neighbor he didn't know watched from his opened window. Minutes ticked by. He wished he'd grabbed his gloves. Liam and his terrier, this time leashed, joined him.

"What happened?" Liam said, taking off his earmuffs.

"They're checking for an intruder." Amir didn't want to talk. He and Liam watched as cops filed out of the house, got in their cruisers, and drove past. Only Officer Nichols stood on the porch. He waved for Amir to return.

"Guess it's safe," Liam said and continued his nightly amble around the neighborhood.

Amir jogged back up the cove. He thought he noticed the hanging swing on the wraparound porch rock back as if someone were sitting on it. He looked at it for a moment, but it was now still.

"No sign of any intruder, Dr. Hadad. Come back in." He opened the front door and motioned for Amir to step inside. "There's no forced entry; everything appears to be in order. We checked the entire home, the garage, the basement. It's all clear."

"But … I heard a man."

"Was a radio or television on? Do you have Alexa? She spooks me all the time."

"Only the television," Amir shook his head. "But I turned it off and heard it again." It wasn't even cold now.

"Could've been your mind tricked you. Don't worry too much, but to give you peace of mind, criminals don't like to be seen. I'd recommend perimeter lights, with motion sensors. You can add security cameras, too, through your home alarm system."

Amir held out his hand. "I'm sorry to have bothered you."

"No bother, doc. That's why we're here. Feel free to call me at the precinct if you notice anything else." At the doorway he turned back. "A dog's a good idea too. Criminals really hate them."

"I'll look into that. Thank you, officer." Amir watched the sedan drive away. Could it have been the television? He was sure he'd turned it off and heard the voice again. Why had it gotten so cold? Was he going crazy? Maybe he was tired, or too stressed with worrying about Camille. He needed a vacation. He would convince Camille to get away with him.

He set the alarm to away, locked the house, and drove to meet his family. He'd get security cameras and perimeter lights installed this week, and Sami had been begging for a dog for months. It might be good for Camille, too. He'd talk it over with her tonight once Sami was in bed. Yes, he thought. A vacation and a dog would be very good, for all of them.

CHAPTER FOUR

···◆◆◆···

*C*amille's car wasn't in the driveway when Amir returned from work the next evening and he hoped she'd restarted her yoga classes. He took off his scrubs, grabbed a clean T-shirt and jeans from the dryer, and entered the kitchen. He knew from the distinct aroma that Sabiha had prepared his favorite dish, Tebeet, the slow-cooked chicken and rice dish seasoned with a blend of Arabic spices called Baharat.

"The house smells like Shabbat," he said as Sami ran into his open arms. "Did you help make dinner, baby girl?"

Sami nodded. "I put pepper."

"She added pepper and paprika." Sabiha stirred the soup on the stove. "Why don't you go play with your new firetruck, let me talk to Daddy? You'll be ready to go if the fire station's alarm sounds. *Yallah.*"

"*Yallah! Voilà!*" Sami giggled and went to find her truck.

Sabiha spoke in Hebrew with a soft voice. "Camille should be back any minute from Trader Joe's. We were out of *shkedeh marak,* or the 'mini croutons,' as Camille calls them." She put the stove on simmer. "Are you going to tell me what happened last night? The police were here?"

"I thought I heard a man in the house, but it was my imagination." Amir kissed his grandmother's cheek. "Don't worry."

"Camille's worried."

"There's a change, huh?"

"What do you mean 'a change'?"

"Did you make Shorba?" Standing next to her at the stove, he sampled the tomato soup Sabiha had eaten as a child in Iraq; it tasted like devotion.

"It's not done." Sabiha shooed him away from her cooking. "Camille thinks of you all the time. Why would you say such a thing?"

"I only meant you and I worry about her so much. That's all."

"What did you hear last night, exactly?"

"You'll think I'm crazy, like the cops." Amir sat on the stool at the counter, feeling like he did as a child watching his mother cook. With his parents' return to Israel last year to be close to his brother's family and his special needs child, he and Sabiha were the last to live in Naperville.

"*Nu?* Are you going to tell me?" Sabiha's gaze was now at eye level.

"I heard a man with an accent." He tore off a piece of challah. "That's all."

"Have you been sleeping, *motek?*" Sabiha studied his face.

"I'm fine, Savtah," he said. "Stop worrying. The cops said to get a dog."

"A dog? That's a good idea." Sabiha turned the stove off. "There are so many that need homes. We could go to Dog Patch and see their rescues."

Sami ran into the kitchen, squealing. "A dog! We get a dog?"

"Who's eavesdropping on the grown-ups?" She gave Amir an apologetic look and playfully swatted Sami's bottom with a dishrag. "Help me set the table, *Yaldah.*"

"A dog! A dog!" Sami hopped up and down.

A gust of cold air breezed inside. "Has a decision been made in Siberia without me?" Camille set the groceries on the counter, took off her coat, and kissed Amir's cheek. Her lips were chilled.

"No, of course not. Savtah and I were talking in Hebrew and the little face understood us. We need to learn a fifth language so we can talk behind her back." He rubbed Camille's bottom, his hands out of Sabiha's vision, hidden by the counter bar top. "Come here, let me warm you."

"Mommy, get dog!" Sami clung to her mother's legs and Amir let go.

Camille bent and kissed Sami, her hair smelled like the fresh-baked challah Amir was devouring. She brushed flour off Sami's Winnie the Pooh T-shirt. "Like I told Daddy last night," she said and glanced at Amir, "a dog will become my responsibility. Daddy is at work all day, and Savtah cannot walk a dog."

"I walk dog, Mommy. My dog." Sami looked up at Camille. "Please, please, please. I want dog."

"I'll walk him before and after work, too." Amir put the groceries away. With his brown eyes and sly grin, he knew how to charm his wife. "It'll be a Hadad family dog. Not just yours."

"I can't walk him, but I'll dog sit anytime," Sabiha said. "You have a huge backyard, he won't always need long walks." Sabiha rummaged in her purse for her phone. "I'll call Dog Patch to arrange for you to see their rescues; is Sunday okay?"

"Sunday! Dog!" Sami ran circles in the kitchen.

Camille lowered her head in defeat.

"Yallah," Sabiha said, a broad smile on her face. "Come, let's light the candles. It's almost Shabbat."

·· • ✦ ◆ ✦ • ··

After Camille read Sami her third Dr. Seuss book, *Green Eggs and Ham,* the child drifted asleep. She kissed her forehead and tucked her in, turning off the bedside light. She found Amir in the den with the paper, doing last Sunday's crossword puzzle. The dinner dishes littered the dining table.

As she loaded the dishwasher, Amir brought more dishes to the sink. "You know, dogs are messy. They shed," she said. "They have accidents. I have a potty-trained child and now I will have dog shit to clean." She kept her back to him.

"Even the way you say *clean* is sexy. I hear that French accent out of those luscious lips, and I dissolve." He wrapped his arms around her from behind, without touching her scar and nuzzled her neck.

His silky hair, like Sami's, weakened her. "Don't be mad," he cooed.

"I cannot give Sami a little sister or brother, so I should at least give her a dog, right?" She turned the water on, rinsing Sami's sippy cup and mumbling in French. "Did you and Sabiha discuss your infertile French wife?"

"Wait wait wait, Pepé Le Pew." He turned off the sink and held both of her hands in his, pulling her against him. "You stop being a stinker. I want a dog for extra protection, hearing that noise spooked me. And I think it will be good for us. I've always had a home with a dog."

"And I have never had one. And never wanted one."

"You don't know what you're missing." He turned her toward him. His eyes gentle. He was so damn handsome, her Iraqi-Israeli-American man.

"Yolanda is coming twice a week, then. I cannot keep this place clean with you two little slobs and a dog."

"Oh my little Pepé, you can have anything you want."

"Except a house with no dog." She slapped his bottom but gave a faint smile. "Can we not go to the Gala?"

"That's something else that will be good for both of us. I need to be there if I'm going to be Chairman. Please? Last favor of the year." He crossed his fingers. "I promise."

"Two hours. We go, you are fawned over, we leave."

"It's fifteen minutes away." He lifted her chin. "At Arista. How about I book a room, make a night of it. You can sleep in, have a spa appointment? Sabiha said she's happy to stay with Sami."

"You two are quite the pair," Camille said, with a playful shake of her head. "No one says no to you and Sabiha; you both should have been in the Mossad."

CHAPTER FIVE

·· · ◆ · ··

*S*abiha held Sami's color chart in the backseat of Camille's Tesla SUV, with its upgraded white upholstery, and practiced with her great-grandchild. Her arthritic fingers ached as she reached for the *sha-sha* she'd hidden under the folds of the child's seat. Her fingers felt the gold amulet from her Iraqi childhood. The amulet resembled a cage encompassing a peanut shell, and was the same size as one as well. It had three pendants dangling from it, each with a turquoise gem. One pendant symbolized God's hand, or Chamtzah, and the other two symbolized eyes.

Camille had shunned the piece as superstitious voodoo and refused to put it over Sami's crib. "There is no such thing as the evil eye, Sabiha. And if there is, well, it already struck us. What is worse than no more children?" Camille wiped the indigo dye off Sami's forehead. "I let you paint her, but that is it. No more rituals on my baby."

Instead of arguing with a distraught mother, Sabiha found this safe hiding place in Sami's car seat. Camille didn't know that when Sabiha was a child in Iraq living along the Tigris River, her grandmother taught her how to combat *ayn*, the evil eye. "The evil eye can bring a man to his grave, and a camel to the cooking pot," her grandmother Massooda, a healer, said over eighty years ago in their home constructed from uneven rocks and cement. "There is much you must learn."

Sabiha stroked the child's hair. Sami reminded her so much of Amir at that age, when they didn't know to put the seat facing backward. Things were a lot different with her children, grandchildren, and great-grandchildren, mostly for the worse. Camille and Amir were bickering about his driving in the front as Sabiha distracted the child. That was different too.

She and Elyass, her husband, had rarely bickered; they had the gratitude of survivors. Despite their families having lived peacefully amongst their Muslim neighbors in Iraq for generations, they witnessed the horrific ethnic cleansing of their community. A mob of Arab nationalists, armed with swords, knives, and guns, burned their synagogue and massacred their Jewish neighbors. Their families fled Iraq on foot to become refugees in Jerusalem.

At moments like these, driving in suburban Chicago past the McDonald's and Taco Bell, she questioned her and Elyass's decisions. Perhaps if they'd stayed in Israel with their only son, instead of uprooting him from his community, her grandson would have more appreciation of their good fortune. He would have a deeper connection to their heritage, she was certain. She didn't mind living among the Germans and Catholics in Naperville, but she was afraid Sami would never understand where she came from. Would she ever be permitted to visit Baghdad? The blood of her ancestors coursed through her, but would Sami ever acknowledge their pain?

"Blue!" Sami said, pointing to the color chart in Sabiha's hand.

"Purple," Sabiha corrected her, though it did look like a deep blue.

"We get pink for dog!" Sami said. She kicked her legs against the back cushion.

They turned onto Ogden Street, passing the Stardust Motel and her pharmacy, where she received her arthritis and hypertension medications. Amir pulled in front of a yellow brick building with a blue awning. The Dog Patch signage had a sketch of a dog sitting by a fire hydrant. Amir parked in front of the metal-fenced yard where a black and white Pit Bull watched them; Camille unbuckled Sami from her seat and let her out. The Pit Bull stood on his hind legs with his paws on the fence. Sami began to run to him, but Amir scooped her into his arms. He pointed to a sign on the fence and read it to Sami.

"We are rescue animals! Please approach us with care, we may be scared in our new environment." He patted her bottom. "We don't pet dogs we do not know, honey. We always need permission."

Camille helped Sabiha out of the car, and retrieved her walker from the trunk. The family entered the building, Sabiha first as Amir opened the door for her. A barrage of sensations surrounded them as they entered Dog Patch. Signs hung from the warehouse rafters––Fish, Dog and Cat Food, Ponds, Crates, Dog Grooming, Reptiles, Birds. The various needs of pet owners filled the space as did the smell of those creatures.

A Labrador, missing a front leg, licked Sabiha's hand and a tabby cat watched her from a perch on the counter. A woman wearing the store's emblem, a dog with the words "Find your rescue at Dog Patch," greeted the family and pulled the three-legged dog away. "Sit, Peg."

"What can we do for you sweetheart?" The woman spoke with Sami who was still in Amir's arms. He'd positioned her like a trophy, cradled and facing away from his chest.

"We get dog!"

"Well that's wonderful. Do you want to see who Puppy Rescue 911 brought us this week?"

She opened the door to the adjacent room. There were twenty dog crates, most of them occupied. "Look and see whom you might want to meet. But don't try and pet one just yet."

Sabiha and Camille watched from the doorway as Amir took Sami from crate to crate. "I wonder which one she'll like," Sabiha said.

"She will want that cocker mix; it looks like Lady from *Lady and the Tramp*," Camille said. "I bet it will shed." Instead, Sami pointed to the golden retriever in the large cage; the tag above his crate read *CHARLIE*. The youthful dog wagged his tail and pawed the crate, excited to play.

"Oomph," Camille said. "She wants that big male dog. He looks dirty."

"Oh he's a very gentle dog, too. You can pet him," the woman said. "I'll let him out."

Sami hugged Charlie. Her delight was palpable. The dog seemed as pleased as the child and licked her on the nose.

"Goldens are great with kids. You'll see," Sabiha said with a reassuring nod. "She has good taste."

Camille's smile was thin lipped. Sabiha knew to keep quiet with this small victory for her great-grandchild.

"Sami, let's go pick supplies while your parents arrange the adoption," Sabiha said, leading the child away. "You said a pink collar, right?"

CHAPTER SIX

"We bought enough for ten dogs," Camille said as they unloaded the car. She and Amir carried in the supplies—dog crate, safety gates, food, and bowls—as Sami gave Charlie a tour of his new home. They'd dropped Sabiha off at home as it was time for her afternoon nap.

"You sleep with me, Charlie," Sami said, and was about to go upstairs.

"Oh no, no, Sami. Charlie will stay downstairs. We bought him a crate. He will sleep there."

"Camille," Amir said.

"What? You want him all over the house? In her bed?"

"That's how dogs live, they become family. Of course he'll sleep with her."

"So why did we buy the crate and the gates?"

"For when we aren't home. For his safety. Dogs can get into things if they aren't supervised. Like kids."

"Fine. But I am not cleaning up his accidents." Camille got her purse. "You get it all settled. I am going to the grocery store to buy human food. Or since dogs and kids are the same, perhaps Sami should eat the Royal Canin too?"

Camille knew she was behaving unfairly, but she didn't give a damn. Amir and Sabiha had shoved the idea of this dog down her throat and now she didn't even have a say as to the house rules. She drove to the store and took her time ambling down each aisle, skipping the section of diapers and pacifiers.

When she returned home Charlie greeted her at the door, sniffing her crotch and then putting both his paws on her chest as Sami came to her.

"Mommy we walked Charlie. He poopy outside."

She put the groceries on the counter and pet him, once. She picked up her child and kissed her cheek. "You are happy, baby?"

"I love him, Mommy."

Amir unloaded the groceries.

"We showed Charlie the neighborhood," he said. "He seems house trained and good on a leash. And tomorrow night the mobile groomer will come. He'll be so cute after a bath, you won't be able to resist his charm."

"You could use a haircut as well." She'd bought the vanilla pudding Amir liked and watched as he opened one. He ate it while standing near the sink and grinned.

She could never stay angry at that face. He knew it, too.

CHAPTER SEVEN

⋅⋅◆⋅⋅

The white lights adorning the trees on the sidewalk reflected upon the snow of the streets. Beautiful, if you weren't freezing to death, Camille thought. The walk from the valet to Hotel Arista's revolving door was far enough to make her shiver. The delicate fabric of her dress provided no warmth, and her strappy heels felt as if she were barefoot. No winter coat could block the cold snap overtaking Chicago's New Year's Eve.

As Amir checked in with the front desk manager, a congenial Bulgarian named D.P., Camille read the upcoming events on the hotel calendar bulletin. The Winter Wonder Afternoon Tea event was in four days while her sister would be visiting. Viva had called Camille that morning to confirm her Friday morning flight. She was on her winter break from NYU and wanted "Sami cuddles."

"Finger Sandwiches, scones, a selection of fancy cakes, tea of your choice ~ Adults $39, children $24." There were so few things to do in the dead of winter with a child, and Sami would love it. She'd reserve three spots before they left.

The bellman escorted them to a corner room on the eleventh floor, and Camille longed to change into the complimentary robe and slippers and curl into bed with Amir. Instead, she sat to freshen her make-up at the spacious bathroom's vanity. She was a doctor's wife, and Amir needed her tonight as he continued his aspirations. One day he could be the AMA president or the White House physician; who knew with Amir? He was always considering what was bigger and better for his career and his family. It was what she'd most admired about him, his ambition. Before she'd become barren, that is. Now she preferred he stay home every night with her and Sami instead of attending board meetings and gala fundraisers.

He came into the bathroom, bent at the waist, and put his head by hers, their reflections in the illuminated round mirror. "You're a trooper for doing this."

"I will do anything for *mon* Amir, *mon amour*... even live with animals."

"I think Charlie's growing on you. You only pretend not to like him." His eyes were playful in the mirror.

"Charlie is a hairy beast. Like you." She dabbed her powder brush on his nose. "Two minutes. I am almost ready to pretend for your hospital."

They took the elevator to the Grand Ballroom, passed the coat check, and could hear the party. The checkered design carpet did little to absorb the sound. A six-piece orchestra played on an ivory-covered stage, and silver lighting and linens decorated the room. The track lighting and modern chandeliers were dim. Votive candles were on the tables with floral bouquets. Middle-aged women wore poorly fitted ballgowns, and most men wore rented tuxedos. Some, clearly already drunk, were stumbling on the parquet dance floor.

Camille took two champagne glasses from a server's tray. "Thank you," she said and flashed her million-dollar smile. The young man blushed. She handed one to Amir and whispered while gesturing to the dancers with a tilt of her head. "My mom would have plenty unkind things to say."

"Yes, she would." He adjusted the silk lapel of his Armani fitted tuxedo. "But we would please Renée. In fact," he pointed to the red-carpet backdrop and photographer in the corner. "Before we leave, we need a picture to prove how sharp we are."

"Dr. Hadad, I wasn't sure you'd make it." The hospital CEO, a tall woman with natural silver hair and a deep voice, Dr. Liz Higbee, greeted him with a clink of her champagne glass. "I finally get to meet the glamorous singer. I've heard so much about you over cafeteria lunches."

"Camille, meet Dr. Higbee. She keeps our hospital afloat."

Camille said, "I heard your job can require wiretapping."

"Heavens, that was a mess my predecessor dealt with, thank goodness. I'm glad you could make it. It's probably a challenge getting a babysitter on New Year's Eve."

"Amir's grandmother practically lives with us," Camille said. "She is happy to stay with Sami."

"A live-in sitter, how fortunate. You should start on baby number two and take advantage of grandma's generosity."

Camille looked away and took a sip of her champagne. Amir rubbed her lower back.

"I must go mingle; you beautiful people enjoy the evening." She waved to someone behind Camille. "Don't forget to sign up for the silent auctions. We have all sorts of generous donations."

Amir kissed her cheek. "I'm sorry, babe. She didn't mean any harm."

"No one ever does." She put her empty glass on a high-top table.

"I'll say hello to a few more people, and then we can dine and dash." He waved to a medical school classmate who was walking toward them. "You remember Ravi?"

"He is the psychiatrist?"

"Yes."

Amir greeted Ravi with a pat on the back. "My friend, it's good to see you."

"How do you keep that thick head of hair?" Ravi said, rubbing his balding one. "Camille, you look beautiful. Neither of you age."

One of the dozens of servers presented them with a tray of appetizers. "These are grilled cheese bites with spicy shredded chicken, and on this side, I have zucchini charred corn fritters."

"Are there more Vietnamese meatballs circulating?" Ravi said as he helped himself to one of each.

"I'll bring you some," the server said and offered the tray to Amir.

Amir took a fritter for himself and handed one to Camille. "Ravi, how's the psych world treating you?"

"Too many stressed out patients these days with this hyper-political climate," he said. "We might need to put Xanax in Lake Michigan's drinking supply."

Camille's gaze fell upon Ravi's dress shoes, dirtied with sleet. "It is a tough job, no? Helping the crazy people?"

Ravi coughed on his grilled cheese. He looked at her. "My patients aren't crazy. They are sad or stressed or have medical issues like psychosis." He shook his head. "What's hard is when treatment fails them."

"Does that happen a lot?" Camille pulled a strand of her hair out of her eye. "The treatment does not help?"

"More often than I prefer. The brain is complicated; the heart as well."

Camille took a bite of the fritter. She caught Ravi studying her and forced a smile.

After Amir and Camille spent time socializing with the mayor, various city council members, and other physicians, they retired to their room. Camille, quite drunk for the first time in years, slipped off her heels as Amir caressed her.

"You were the most beautiful person in the room, as always," he said.

"That Lexi you work with, I think *she* was the most beautiful, no?" Camille had noticed the woman in the backless gown, sizing up her pinup figure and long hair. She didn't appear to have a date, and various men encircled her most of the night. When Amir had introduced them, she'd noticed an undercurrent of attraction––Lexi to him. Like most women.

"Lexi? She's pretty." His muscular arms pulled her gown up, and she lifted her arms to undress. "But all I ever see is you. All I ever want is you."

The familiar feel of his body, his scent, ignited her, and she pressed her firm body against him. They fell into an intimate and passionate pattern, and she allowed herself to move into his touch. She wrapped her legs around him and he carried her to the bed. She climaxed twice before he did. But afterward, lying on his chest as he slept, the CEO's words, "start on baby number two," played continuously in her mind. Sex was only to show love now.

All the doctors, nurses, and administrators celebrated a new year, a new beginning, but her new beginnings were in the past because of these so-called "Healing Heroes." They'd sliced her life force out as she lay anesthetized. It had happened so fast, the memory a blur.

She'd pushed Sami out; the epidural had worn off enough so she could feel pain. But when her newborn took her first breath and cried, Camille had felt such exquisite joy. With her legs still in stirrups as the obstetrician worked, she held the baby to her breast for the first time. Sami latched on immediately, and Amir kissed the baby and Camille's forehead. "You did so great," he said. "Look how perfect she is."

The nurses didn't look as pleased as they pressed her belly, "massaging" her uterus to stop the vaginal bleeding. Blood poured out of her––she could feel it gushing onto her bottom, but with her legs in stirrups, couldn't see how much. When they took Sami off her breast, mother and child both started to cry. Camille looked at Amir, who had concern in his eyes.

"We have to stop this bleed, Camille," her obstetrician said. "The placenta is out, but the uterus won't clamp down. We need to go to the OR." Within minutes, the team wheeled her into the operating room, without her baby, and without Amir. The anesthesiologist, a woman with kind eyes who had placed the epidural hours earlier, told her to take a deep breath of oxygen, and that was all she remembered.

"Uterine atony," Amir explained when she awoke in the ICU. "They couldn't stop the bleeding and had to do an emergency hysterectomy to save your life. They removed your uterus, honey. They had no choice." He put the railing down, crawled into her hospital bed, and wrapped his arms around her as she wailed. Her sister, grief-stricken, stood at the sliding door, rocking Sami in her arms.

"It'll be okay, *motek,* it'll be okay." Amir held her head under his chin, stroking her. "You're alive, and our daughter is perfect. That's all that matters."

Now, more than two years later, as she felt Amir's chest rise and fall, anger and grief battled within her. His specialty was uterine bleeding, yet he hadn't stopped hers. She didn't fall asleep until dawn.

CHAPTER EIGHT

⸻ ◆ ◆ ⸻

*A*mir spoke with rapid-fire expertise into the handheld Dictaphone, which reminded him of Sami's walkie-talkie, as he read the final overnight chest X-rays from the ICU. The radiology reading room was empty and its overhead lights were permanently off. He sipped coffee from the doctor's lounge and opened the CT scans. As the first one loaded, he reflected on New Year's Day. His hope that a vacation might lift Camille's mood had been extinguished. She had seemed even sadder in the morning. She had no interest in a spa treatment or brunch, so they'd packed and gone home. Only when reunited with Sami did Camille's smile return.

"Happy New Year, Amir." Wearing scrubs, Jade hung her white lab coat on a wall hook and took a seat at the workstation next to him. "I've got a paracentesis in the unit waiting for me. Are you doing the nephrostomy?" She pulled up an image.

"I need consent from the family. I think the OR has it at two o'clock," he said. "That reminds me…" He dialed a number on a house phone. "Miss Dee, I'll need the C-arm and Phillips ultrasound for that case this afternoon."

Amir hung up and focused on the X-ray image of a long bone. He held the Dictaphone near his lips and spoke with a soft voice. "Clinical background 'Status post fall.' There is an intertrochanteric fracture in the right femur bone…"

Wouldn't want old mother to trip. Break a hip.

Black smoke circled and hovered in front of his screen—cold, damp smoke. He shoved the desk, rolling his chair away. It happened rapidly, almost too fast for him to comprehend. He heard organ music as though he were in a cathedral.

The man's voice returned––clearer and louder than ever.

Bury my bones, you bleedin' thieves.

Amir's Dictaphone dropped as he jumped up from his seat. He fumbled in the dark and found the switch to flip on the overhead lights.

"Why'd you do that!" Jade said, squinting.

"Did you hear that?" Amir said.

"Hear what?"

Amir put his finger to his lips. The smoke had evaporated. Amir felt himself hyperventilating and gripped the chair to keep from passing out. He was going insane, he thought. This was psychosis.

"Sit." Jade rubbed his back and guided him into his chair. She held his wrist feeling his pulse. She crouched by him. "Breathe. Slow, deep breaths. Are you having chest pain?"

Amir shook his head. He slowed his breath.

"You're having a panic attack. My brother has these. Just breathe, Amir. It'll end soon."

If only it was a panic attack, he thought. He was much more ill. Maybe he had a tumor in his head from all the radiation of the job. A colleague had recently passed from glioblastoma. He thought of Camille and her overwhelming depression. This would do her in. He couldn't tell her until he knew what his diagnosis and prognosis were.

"It's passed. I'm going to go wash my face." He held Jade's hand for a fleeting moment. "If you could keep this between us…"

"It's nothing to be ashamed of," Jade said. "But of course, it's no one's business. I'm here if you need."

Amir flipped the overhead lights off as he walked out and called Ravi.

·· ✦ ✦ ✦ ✦ ··

Amir managed to complete the workday and take care of his patients. After he'd read the last image, he called Camille to say he was running late in the OR and not to wait on him for dinner. It was six o'clock, but so dark it could've been midnight, as he drove to Naperville Executive Court on Iroquois Street. Dr. Ravi Patel's office was housed next to a childcare service and a chiropractor center in a three-story office building with a domed sunroof over the lobby. Since it was after hours, the chance anyone would recognize him was slim as he parked his car in the lot. There were only three other cars there.

Amir pulled the front glass door to enter, but it was locked. He knocked on the glass panel under the brown awning and peered inside at the potted trees under the sunroof. There was no one in the hallway. He pulled off his gloves and texted Ravi.

I'm out front. Door is locked.

…

Be right there.

Ravi unlocked and opened the door. "Please come in. I forgot they lock it so early." Ravi led him past the restrooms and water fountain and through the vacant waiting room. The staff was gone for the day, and the lights were off in the nurse's station. "Please." He motioned for Amir to enter his office and offered him a seat on the couch across from his upholstered chair. There was a water bottle and a box of Kleenex on the coffee table between them. Amir hung his coat on the rack by the door and sat.

It still surprised him at times to see his classmates as real doctors, in private practice with spouses and kids. Amir remembered Ravi, when they *both* had a full head of hair, dancing with Ali at a party their first weeks in medical school. Ravi was surprisingly smooth on the dance floor, he recalled.

"What's on your mind, Amir?" Ravi picked up a yellow note pad and pen.

"For the past couple of weeks, I've been hearing voices. Well actually, one voice. It's scaring the hell out of me."

"Tell me more." Ravi took notes; his pen moved quickly. "What's the voice saying?"

"It's a man, foreign. Perhaps Irish."

"Is the voice familiar? Is it telling you to harm yourself or others?"

"No, nothing like that." He told Ravi the details of the incidents, starting with the shower and ending with that day's in the reading room. "When the smoke appeared, I knew I needed to get help. I want a CT to rule out an organic brain lesion; it's likely occipital."

"I'll order a CT of the head, we do need to rule that out. Although it's quite unusual to have auditory and visual hallucinations attributed to a brain lesion, with no other concomitant symptoms. Amir, tell me. What stressors are happening in your life? Is there something going on at home? I sensed grief from Camille."

Amir sank further into the couch, and rested his head against the cushion. "Not more than anyone else's home."

"Like what, for example, is similar to anyone else's home?"

"Camille is struggling. That's been hard."

"What's she struggling with?"

Amir closed his eyes. He didn't want to betray Camille.

"Amir, what's Camille struggling with?"

"She needed an emergent hysterectomy for uterine atony when Sami was born. She can't seem to move past the initial stages of grief. It's hard to see her so sad. And I think she blames me for not stopping the bleed myself."

"Do you blame yourself as well?"

"Maybe I do. I stop uterine bleeding as a subspecialty. Yet my wife almost bled to death."

"But she didn't bleed to death. She survived."

"I'm not sure she sees it that way."

"Here's what I'd like to do. I'm going to order a panel of labs… electrolytes, TSH, urinalysis, tox screen, liver enzymes, thiamine, B12 and folate, and HIV. Let's get the head CT as soon as possible, though that tends to be low yield with no neurological symptoms. I'll call you with a time and place once it's pre-certed and scheduled. I'm going to hold off any medication for now, as atypical antipsychotics can have significant side effects. You and I should meet weekly. With Camille as well, if she would be amenable."

"I'd prefer without her."

"I feel she needs to be involved. You have my personal cell, and it is with me at all hours. If the voice returns, call me immediately. If there is ever suicidal ideation you need to call me as well."

"I'm not suicidal, Ravi." Amir stood and put on his coat. "I might have glioblastoma, but I'm not suicidal."

"We'll figure it out. Bring Camille."

CHAPTER NINE

⸻ · ◆ · ⸻

Viva, a radiant, dark-complexioned version of her big sister, with almond eyes and chestnut hair, brushed the snow off her winter coat as Camille wriggled Sami out of hers. The Hotel Arista's heat enveloped them as they walked through the lobby and Sami scampered to the white Christmas tree still in the lounge.

"Santa here?" Sami squealed, caressing an oversized holiday gift box under the tree.

"She knows she's Jewish, right?" Viva, speaking French, laughed.

"What can I tell you, he never got to meet her, but Dad's genes are alive and well." Camille picked Sami up. "Christmas is over *ma poupée,* my little doll. They just have not taken down their tree."

"Welcome." The Che Figata hostess was dressed in all black except for a Santa hat. She escorted them to a semi-circular table for their afternoon tea service and smiled at Sami. Technically, Sami was too young for the Afternoon Tea event, but the hostess didn't mind. "Does she need a booster?"

The Italian restaurant, also still decorated with white LED string lights, was at capacity, and the sound of merriment surrounded them. Their table overlooked the open kitchen with a wood-fire pizza oven. Italian music played in the ceiling speakers. Once Sami was situated, the waitress appeared with an array of finger sandwiches. "From Italy to table," she said. She offered the sisters prosecco and Sami sparkling apple cider.

"Momma is blueberry." Sami held up her scone. Half of the scone, it seemed, was crumbling on her child's ballerina dress; but the matching purple hairband kept her hair off her face and out of her food.

Camille bit into a miniature tiramisu; its filling oozed in her mouth. "How're things with Devin?" she said, in French. "Are things better?"

"They want me to meet the parents, and I'm so not interested. I think we should open it up, date others. They aren't having it, though." Viva shrugged. "Might be time to move on."

"You young people," Camille said. "With the fluidity and open relationships."

"What can I tell you, sis. We're not as traditional as you and Amir." She smiled. "Speaking of non-traditional..." Viva pulled a pamphlet out of her purse and slid it across the table. A silhouette of a headless pregnant woman's body was on the front. Since they continued to speak in French, Sami didn't understand. "It's called gestational surrogacy, and it's legal here," Viva said. "Your egg, Amir's sperm. I can be the pouch."

Camille read the front. "The American Society of Reproductive Medicine." Tears welled in her eyes as she continued reading in silence. Surrogacy was banned in France, but very few believed it should be. Camille would never pay a woman for her body, considering it a type of prostitution. To abuse a stranger's body for forty weeks and change her physically forever, possibly scarring her emotionally as well, was unthinkable to her. It never occurred to Camille to ask her sister, to *risk* her sister.

"I couldn't possibly ask this..."

"You aren't asking. I'm offering," Viva reached across the table and grasped her hand. "I want to give you this gift and give Sami a sibling."

"What if..." Camille squeezed her hand. "What if what happened to me happens to you? Or worse."

Sami kicked her legs against the booth's blue velvet cushions, and watching her mother's tears, tried to console her. "Momma happy. I happy."

Camille took Sami out of her booster and onto her lap. She hugged her to her chest. "Momma is happy. I missed Tante Viva, is all."

"We could do it over spring break," Viva continued in French. "I'll have one more year in my master's program; it's perfect timing to cook a baby for you. I know it's a lot to consider, Sis, but talk it over with Amir. You'll need to begin injecting hormones soon for egg retrieval."

Camille bounced Sami on her knees. "I don't know. I have to think about it. Amir's been distant the past couple of days..."

"How so?"

"He said work's been busy, but I'm not convinced."

"Did you have a disagreement?" She licked at a cannoli and made a face while swooning, her hand over her forehead, which made Sami giggle. "Napervillians are lucky to have yummy Italy down the street."

"We went to a gala here on New Year's Eve, and he wanted me to be bubbly and happy and in 'vacation mode,' but I am not any of those things anymore. He sulked instead of cutting me some slack."

The waitress refilled their prosecco. "Can I get you anything else?"

Viva shook her head and waited until they were alone. "He hasn't experienced the same loss, Camille. He can't understand it as a woman can."

Camille put the pamphlet in her purse. "He thinks Charlie is Sami's sibling."

"He is. But she needs a human one, too. Pick the right time, perhaps in a negligée, and broach the topic. You can be very convincing."

"You are the greatest sister in the universe for offering such a gift, but I don't think this is an option for us."

"Don't say no yet. Think about it."

CHAPTER TEN

·⋅⋅+⋅+◆+⋅+⋅⋅·

*A*s Camille and Viva sipped prosecco at Che Figata, Amir was leaving work early. Miss Dee had scheduled him for a half-day per his request. "I have some important meetings I need to attend," he'd explained. After changing out of scrubs and into jeans and a sweater, he drove down the block to the hospital's outpatient facility and checked in with the other patients. The staff didn't know him by name. Anonymity was a luxury most in healthcare weren't afforded, but one offered to radiologists.

The waiting room had immaculate linoleum floors and brightly cushioned seats. Some were extra-large to accommodate the girth of middle Americans. He took a seat in the far corner, and his foot tapped as he read the news on his phone. The government shutdown had no end in sight, but at least there was a familiar face as Speaker of the House again; he agreed with Camille, if women ran the government, education would soar, war and crime would plummet.

"Dr. Hadad?" A youthful female technician in scrubs, holding a manila file, called from the doorway.

Amir stood and motioned to her, and her expression warmed as he approached.

"Dr. Hadad?" Her voice softer as her gaze took him in. She smoothed her hair.

"Amir."

"Right this way." She swept her arm.

Amir positioned himself on the CT scanner bed with his head near the cylindrical gantry. The technician handed him a hand control with a red button. "Push this and we can hear you in the control room."

"Got it."

He held as still as possible, wanting minimal artifact on the images. As the machine slid him further inside, he held his breath. He knew his chances for a malignancy were higher than an average patient his age, due to all the radiation his job exposed him to. But a tumor was possibly curable. Schizophrenia never seemed to be.

When the scan was complete, he asked the technician for a copy of the disk, explaining his specialty.

"Of course, Dr. Hadad. I'll get that for you." She disappeared into the control room as he waited in the hallway. Returning a few minutes later, her hand brushed his as she handed it to him. She blushed.

He thanked her and strode to the parking lot, eager to get home and read it before his family returned.

···✦✦✦✦✦···

Amir was greeted by Charlie when he entered the kitchen. The dog stood on his hind legs and pressed his paws onto Amir's chest, licking his face and grunting.

"Good boy, Charlie. Down." He petted the dog and unlatched the gate at the kitchen entrance. "Come, let's get to work." Amir went to his office down the hall from the master bedroom as Charlie followed, his tail wagging.

Amir's reading room was as professional and clean as the hospital's. It was a strict "no Sami" zone. He sat, inserted the disk in the reader, and watched the images load. He'd never studied his own brain before. He noted the familiar gray and black structures, and scrolled through slice by slice as he would for any patient. He hovered at the mid-level, and looked closer at the left cerebellopontine angle. There was gray where white should be, and it might explain auditory and visual hallucinations. At less than a millimeter in length, it could be the beginning of a lesion or it could be artifact. He'd need an MRI to confirm. He read the rest of the film and it was otherwise clean. He wondered how an objective radiologist would read it. He texted Jade.

Can you take a moment to read a head CT.

...

Sure. What's the name?

...

It's mine. Panic attack work up. 08/20/1981.

...

Pulling it up now.

A few minutes passed, then his cell phone rang. Jade was on the other end. "I recommend an MRI," she said. "I'm seeing a possible lesion at the left cerebellum, but it's likely artifact. Fortunately, there's no hydrocephalus or mass shift."

"I concur."

"Are you having any issues with balance? Hearing loss?"

"No issue with balance, but there is some... irregular auditory noise." He coughed. Charlie whimpered and pawed for attention. "I'll get the MRI."

"Let me know, I'll read it."

"Will do." Amir put on his heaviest coat and leashed Charlie. He put the Bluetooth ear piece in, called Ravi, and updated him as he walked the dog.

"I understand," Ravi said. "I'll schedule an MRI. I just pulled up your labs, all are normal. Only the tox screen for heavy metals is pending."

This is where I hanged.

The voice, the Irishman. Amir yanked the Bluetooth ear piece out. He rubbed his ear and put the phone on speaker. "We've got to figure this out, Ravi. I just heard the voice as clearly as if you were speaking to me."

"Same singular voice?"

"Same Irish asshole."

"Come to my office Monday, six o'clock. And bring Camille."

Charlie, his muzzle pointed away from Amir, began growling, then barking at the new construction site on Chicago Avenue. He bared his teeth. "Whoa, boy. What's wrong?" Amir followed the dog's gaze to the bottom of the hill and saw only the sign for a future condominium to be called "Chicago Commons." A car turned off Chicago Avenue and drove past them on Huffman Street. The sidewalks were vacant.

Charlie whimpered. He sat at Amir's feet, and pawed him. Amir crouched and patted his back. "It's okay, boy, we're all a bit spooked these days. Let's get home for Shabbat."

CHAPTER ELEVEN

Ravi returned to the stovetop to stir the daal he was cooking. The twins loved his yellow lentil dish, a family recipe passed on for three generations. Ali was slicing onions and lemons next to him to serve on the side for her parents.

"Who's Camille?" she said, tilting her head toward the smartphone. "You look worried."

"I am, a bit." Ravi reached over her head and rummaged for chili peppers in their spice cabinet. "My med school classmate, Amir, you might remember him? He's having symptoms that don't make any sense."

"Tell me," Ali said.

Ravi explained Amir's symptoms. "The Irish voice is so random, and the visual hallucination with it… I've never seen or read of such a patient presentation."

Ali had her doctorate in Biology and taught at North Central College, a five-minute walk from their downtown home. Her lustrous hair was in a long ponytail. From behind, she looked as she had at New Trier High School, a suburban school they'd both attended. Being two years her junior, Ravi hadn't had the nerve to ask her out and was too shy to befriend her, despite being one of only a handful of kids of Indian heritage in the school. Years later, he got his chance when his parents arranged a meeting. "Not an arranged marriage," his mother insisted. "Just an arranged date." He didn't need convincing.

Ali had been charming, beautiful, and full of laughter as their coffee date morphed into a dinner date. He was mesmerized by her smile. The fact she said yes to his marriage proposal three months later was a miracle to him. He only wished their sex life was more robust. He couldn't remember the last time she'd initiated it. Their marriage counselor advised monthly "dates," but even those were becoming fewer.

Ali put the knife down and arranged the onions and lemon next to the chili peppers on a serving dish. "It sounds more like a ghost, a *bhoot*."

Ravi tilted his head. "Why would a *bhoot* be haunting him? And an Irish one, at that? That's not very scientific of you." Ravi patted her bottom.

"Sometimes science doesn't have the answers." She moved out of his reach. "You chose matters of the mind, the least scientific of all specialties."

"A ghost, though? I think a more logical explanation involves brain chemistry and stress."

Their twin sons ran into the kitchen, and while chasing one another, knocked over a flower vase. "Boys, go to the playroom until dinner is ready. Shoo," Ali said while picking the plastic vase off the floor.

Ravi knelt and gathered the tulips he'd brought her. Flowers in the dreary winter were a luxury she appreciated. He grabbed a towel to soak the water off the faux wood flooring.

"Well, that Irish voice sounds demonic, if you ask me," she stood and rearranged the tulips in a new vase. "Be careful not to get too involved with this Irishman and Amir."

Ravi heard the front door unlock, and her parents shouted greetings as their boys ran to them. He shot Ali a look and whispered, "I thought we decided no keys."

"*You* decided no keys. They decided otherwise." She wiped her hands on his apron and went to greet her parents.

Enmeshment, he thought. His wife didn't see it but her parents needed boundaries. He returned to the daal and considered if it was a battle worth revisiting.

CHAPTER TWELVE

⋅⋅◆◆◆⋅⋅

"Tante Viva was so sweet to get us these tickets!" Camille said, watching Sami bounce in her seat with excitement. She, Sami, Viva, and Sabiha sat in the third row in the Paramount Aurora Theater as the curtains closed for intermission on the *Wizard of Oz* matinee. The restored Art Deco palace from the 1930s had luxurious reupholstered original seats, floor-to-ceiling hand-painted murals, and chandeliers dating back to the initial build.

She only wished Amir had joined them; instead, he was working from home, having given his ticket to Sabiha at Shabbat dinner last night. "You ladies enjoy," he'd said, kissing her cheek over coffee this morning.

Sami knew all the songs by heart and squealed as Dorothy danced with the Lion and Tin Man. "Charlie!" Like many of the children, she stood in her seat when the live dog was on stage.

"Time to potty?" Camille pushed Sami's velvety hair out of her eyes.

"I'll take her," Viva said with an extended hand, her voice imitating the Wicked Witch. "Come with me, my pretty little Munchkin."

"Eeee!" Sami giggled and followed her down the crowded aisle of parents and kids. Camille watched Viva pick her up, and as Sami's arms encircled her sister, Camille felt a wave of gratitude. Sabiha and Viva were surrogate mothers to Sami; they loved her as much as she did. Perhaps Viva being an actual surrogate wasn't too implausible.

Turning to speak over Viva and Sami's vacant seats, she skipped small talk. Sabiha was candid and honest, like most Israelis Camille knew.

"Have you noticed Amir acting funny?" Camille said, picking Sami's coat off the floor. "Ever since the night he called the cops, he seems… distracted."

"I've wanted to ask you the same thing, *motek* dear. I noticed last night he seemed troubled." Sabiha's walker was folded and propped in front of her. She rested her arthritic hands on it. "He told me he was tired."

"He is restless at night. I have noticed him not sleeping well." Maybe that was all it was, she thought.

"Insomnia?"

"Yes."

"He needs to eat more. He eats like a little bird. Feed him a big meal and get him some melatonin. Make sure he has socks on his feet in bed."

"Should I read him a bedtime story like Sami?" Camille smiled.

"I think you could tire him out another way." They both laughed. "Once he has a few good nights' rest, I bet he will be fine." She reached and patted Camille's arm for emphasis. "Don't worry."

Camille debated discussing the idea of Viva's surrogacy with Sabiha, but she was already treated differently because of the trauma she'd been through. She didn't want more sympathy and didn't know what her elder would think. Would she adamantly oppose or encourage it? An intrusive thought repeated: what if Amir, in the future, decided he *did* want more children? She was certain plenty of women, like that Lexi in her backless dress, would be happy to make his babies.

Sami came down the aisle ahead of Viva. "What's the *craic*?" Sami said, handing her mom the ruby slippers Viva had bought her at the concession stand. "What's the *craic*, what's the *craic*?" She giggled with excitement.

"Where did you learn Irish? Viva, did you teach her that?" Camille was laughing as she undid Sami's shoes to exchange them with the slippers.

"The child knows Hebrew, Arabic, American English, and French. Why should I teach her Irish?"

"Sami, where did you learn the word *craic*?"

"Patrick."

Camille studied her daughter. "Who is Patrick?"

"My friend."

Camille glanced at Viva and Sabiha, shrugging her shoulders with an exaggerated frown. "We do not know a Patrick, *ma poupée*."

"Ah, she already has imaginary friends. Only the brightest children have imaginary friends so young." Sabiha kissed her forehead. "Time for you to go play with real friends at nursery school, I say."

CHAPTER THIRTEEN

⸱⸱✦✦✦⸱⸱

*A*mir finished his Monday morning list in the reading room at the hospital, ending with MRIs so he could focus on them. Afterward, he ate the complimentary lunch at the doctor's cafeteria, sitting alone, and reading *The Daily Herald.* Glancing up, he was surprised to see Lexi scan her badge and enter. Someone in security must've granted her special access. He figured a woman like her was given many favors from men. In his younger years, he might've pursued her as well. She exuded sex with every sway of her hip. He continued reading the newspaper. Those bachelor days were over.

"May I join you?" Lexi appeared holding a tray, a plate on it piled with vegetables and chicken.

He extended his hand to the other chair.

"I'll be assisting on the chemoembolization this afternoon. I didn't see an order for pharmacy. Which agent will you need?" She took a bite of her carrots while pushing the peas aside.

"I'll confer with Heme Onc; they usually put in the order. Thanks for the early catch." He watched her play with her food. "Are you doing surgery on your peas and carrots?"

She laughed. "No idea why peas and carrots are a thing, right? Why can't I have only carrots?" She tucked a long tendril of her glossy hair behind her ear and looked at Amir.

Amir knew that look. He stood. "I'll get that order resolved, pharmacy needs time with chemo drugs." He walked briskly away from her. As he stacked his plate and tray in the dirty bin he felt a pat on his back. Startled, he dropped his glass in the bin.

"Amir," Liz Higbee said, her low voice higher than usual, "I didn't mean to sneak up on you." She peered into the bin and at his hands.

"I'm surprised that didn't break," Amir said.

"I'll be sure not to surprise you in the O.R." Her face held a smile. "Especially now that you're Chairman."

"Am I?" Amir smiled.

"Votes are tallied. I knew you were a natural leader when I recruited you. I'll be seeing you at the monthly medical executive committee. Our next one is in three weeks."

"It'll be my honor." Amir gave a slight bow but his unease grew, thinking of what could be growing inside his skull.

···◆◆◆◆···

After the chemoembolization case, Amir went for his MRI in the outpatient facility. He felt a knot in his throat thinking of Sami. The MRI tech handed Amir ear plugs. "It gets hot and loud in there," he said. "You'll want to push these in before you lie down." Amir obliged and then rested his head on the foam cushion. The tech locked a semicircular plastic headpiece over Amir's head and face, caging him still.

"You okay?" He placed a hand device rod in Amir's palm. "Push this button anytime to speak with me. I can hear and see you. If you look up, you can see my reflection in the mirror by your head."

"Got it," Amir said.

The narrow sides forced him to keep his hands on his abdomen and it felt restricting as the tech slid him deeper into the tube. It was significantly more confining than the CT scanner and Amir knew why claustrophobic patients needed general anesthesia to get into one. The noise from the machine sounded like muffled electronic dance music from the clubs he visited with Camille in college. To distract himself, he closed his eyes and recalled those earlier years with her.

He'd first spotted her walking across the quad his junior year of college. Her gait was more of a glide, with those long dancer's legs. He'd sprinted to catch up with her. She was even more striking up close, with flawless skin and a dab of red lip gloss, like a Hollywood glamour girl from the golden era. And then, she'd spoken. Her voice, her accent, her laugh. It was over for him; he was hers.

Their chemistry had been electric, and she'd been insatiable in those earlier years. They married after his first year of medical school, honeymooning in Italy. Their rented villa had an infinity pool, and they didn't see much of Tuscany, as he recalled.

"I wonder if they have cameras recording us," she'd said kissing him in the pool. He'd held her bottom as her legs wrapped around him under water.

"Would you like that?" he said.

"I like to only pretend we are being watched," she murmured nibbling on his ear lobe. "I think it is there." She pointed to a light fixture on the outside of the villa that could easily hide a camera. "Untie my top." He did as told, and watched as she stood topless in the shallow end. She pulled down her bikini and bent her bottom toward the designated "camera."

He was mesmerized as she beckoned him to join her. Afterward, she giggled with the same abandon and said, "Can you believe your wife is so, what is the English word, *naughty?*"

"Why do you think I married her?"

He missed that Camille. That sexy, carefree French goddess. He didn't mind her scar, her infertility. It only made her more beautiful, more real. He'd kiss her wounded belly. "That's a warrior scar, *motek.*" Her sad eyes refused to accept his words.

The MRI made a noise like a thunder clap and Amir opened his eyes. It really felt like a coffin, as he'd heard from numerous patients over the years. He pushed the button in his palm, to ask how much longer he'd be in, but no one answered.

I deserved a bleedin' coffin.

He felt his heart race and pushed the button harder. He looked into the mirror and saw inside the control room. The tech was laughing with a young woman and neither was watching him. He kicked his legs, creating artifact on the image in an effort to get their attention.

"Hey!" Amir screamed and wiggled while pressing the button. He kicked both legs up.

"Whoa, whoa Dr. Hadad ... hold on. I'm coming to get you out." Amir heard the tech's voice in the speaker. The noise from the machine stopped and he heard the heavy door to the room being pushed open. The tech slid him out of the tube and rapidly unlocked the headpiece.

"You okay?" He offered his hand to help Amir sit up.

Amir was panting as sweat poured from his forehead. The thick hair framing his face was damp. He took the tech's hand and sat, his legs dangling from the patient table.

"Calm your breath doc, this happens all the time." He handed him the washcloth the other tech brought in and Amir patted his forehead with it, wiping the sweat away as he slowed his breath.

"We got the images, doc, you don't need to go back in."

Amir nodded. He needed those images.

CHAPTER FOURTEEN

⋯⋅✦⋅⋯

Ravi, seated across from Amir in his office with hands clasped on his knees, leaned forward. "I thought Camille would be joining us tonight."

"I didn't want to involve her until I knew what the MRI showed," Amir said. "I read it and my partner reviewed it… It's negative. This damn voice isn't going to be treated surgically."

"Medicine. We can treat this medically. But we must include Camille."

"Ravi. You know me…"

"I know everything about your presentation is atypical. However, your family has undergone a great deal of stress with Camille's traumatic infertility. Stress wreaks havoc on our bodies and on our minds. I can't treat you in a vacuum: I need to address issues with you and your wife."

Men with soft hands don't know stress.

Amir pushed his hands against his ears. "Stop! Stop!" He rocked in his chair.

"Take a deep breath, Amir. We're going to treat this," Ravi said. "Breathe."

Amir opened his eyes, tears had formed. "I can't be sick. My family needs me."

"What did you experience, just now?"

"He sounded threatening."

"Are you feeling violent? Do you want to hurt me or yourself?"

"Of course not! I just want this voice to go away!"

Ravi went to his desk, wrote on a prescription pad and handed the script to Amir. "I want you to start on low dose risperidone; I have samples in the drug cabinet I will give you to take right away."

Amir put the prescription in his wallet while Ravi stepped out of the room. There must be an explanation for new onset hallucinations besides psychosis, he reasoned. He wasn't insane, for crying out loud.

Ravi returned with a sample vial and a glass of water. "Take it at the same time, every day." He listed the possible side effects, including insomnia, impotence, weight gain, and the dreaded involuntary movements of tardive dyskinesia. "This is the lowest dose possible."

Amir twisted off the top of the vial and took a pill.

"You call me anytime, at any hour if you feel violent toward yourself or others. Next week, I want to see you here with Camille. No excuses."

"I'll do anything. Just make it stop."

CHAPTER FIFTEEN

⋯·⋅◆⋅·⋯

*C*amille and Sami spent Monday afternoon with Viva at the Morton Arboretum. Sami loved playing hide and seek in the maze garden; they were bundled in heavy coats, hats, and scarves as the winter weather was still intense, but enjoyed it for fifteen minutes. It wasn't very crowded, since the cold spell kept families away. Sami would laugh every time Viva read her a posted joke in the Children's Discovery Gardens.

"What did one autumn leaf say to another?" Viva said. "I'm falling for you!" Sami would squeal with laughter and run to the next joke.

"What this one say?" she pointed to the orange sign.

"What kind of tree can fit into your hand? A palm tree!" Viva read aloud and put her hand in Sami's gloved palm.

"It is too cold," Camille said. "Look, her cheeks are flushed. Let us go see the enchanted railroad exhibit inside now."

Camille watched as Viva and Sami walked around the extensive train exhibit and stifled a laugh when Viva promised to buy Sami a train set.

"You realize you're spoiling her," Camille said in French as they sipped hot chocolate in the Arboretum's Ginkgo Restaurant overlooking the frozen lake. The sun was out, and light poured through the floor-to-ceiling windows.

"She's my only niece, of course, I…" Viva stopped speaking when she saw Camille grimace. "Oh, I'm sorry. I didn't mean…"

"It's okay. I know." Camille forced a smile. "I'm used to it. She switched back to English. "You ready for a little nap in the car? We have to take Tante Viva to the airport."

"No. Viva stay," Sami said. "No plane."

55

"I'll visit you soon, my little Munchkin. I promise." Viva said.

·· ◆ ◆ ◆ ◆ ·· ·

Sami cried, saying goodbye to her aunt outside O'Hare Airport's drop off, her legs and arms wrapped tightly around her. Viva kissed her entire face until Sami finally let go. She'd fallen asleep in her car seat from the airport, so Camille skipped the nighttime bath ritual and instead tucked her sleeping girl in bed still wearing her jeans. She'd probably have a nighttime accident, but a wet bed was better than a fussy, cranky toddler.

Camille prepared a heavy meal, trusting in Sabiha's intuition. If Amir needed a full stomach to sleep, she was going to help. He was late again tonight, his work schedule atypical the past two weeks. His evening OR cases and weekend image readings caused her concern. Was Lexi working these late hours, too?

She heard the automatic garage door open and set the frying pan on high. She listened as Amir put his scrubs in the washing machine and hung his car keys on the hook in the laundry room. "Down boy," he said. She could hear Charlie's tail wagging, knocking against the door frame.

"Amir *Amour*," she purred, glancing up from the steak she was searing for him. "I'm glad you're home." Charlie was on his hind legs pawing Amir, almost reaching his face, but Amir's expression was sad. His jaw was clenched. She turned the stove off and went to him.

"What's wrong?" She ran her hands through his thick hair and lifted his chin. He looked as if he'd been crying. "What is it?"

Amir pulled her to him and embraced her, his arms tight, as if he were afraid she wouldn't stay. He buried his head in her hair. "Just a bad day. I'm not feeling well."

"Did something happen?"

"No," he said, releasing his grip. "Where's Sami?"

"I already put her to bed." Camille pulled back and looked into his eyes. She wasn't used to Amir being upset. He was her eternal optimist. "I made you potatoes, salad; I have a steak to finish searing for you. You hungry?"

"Sure *motek*, I can eat," Amir said as Charlie licked his hand. "I should walk him, though."

"Come. Eat first." She led him in his boxers to the dining table and poured them some wine.

"Viva left?" He sat looking up at her.

"You should have seen Sami say goodbye to her. She was pitiful."

"Viva or Sami?"

"Both." She went to the kitchen, returned with two full plates, then sat next to him. "It is a total love fest with those two. In fact…"

"What?"

"Nothing, it can wait."

They ate together in silence for a while, and she watched as Amir's jaw relaxed. She poured him another glass of wine.

"What did you want to tell me?" he said.

Camille studied his expression, unsure, but her sister's offer wouldn't be available for long. Soon she'd graduate, and then who knew where and with whom Viva would be.

"My sister is a junior mom to Sami. Practically a surrogate mother."

"Yeah, she loves our girl."

Camille could see his spirits were lifted as they spoke of Sami. She took a deep breath. "Viva offered to be our actual surrogate. To give Sami a sibling."

Amir put down his wine glass and leaned into the back cushion of his chair. "Surrogacy?"

"Yes, I have information…" Camille went to the kitchen and retrieved the pamphlet from her purse. "It is a good option for us." She handed it to him and sat next to him. "To have another baby."

"Why, Camille?" Amir looked at the pamphlet and shook his head. "Why can't this be enough?" He raised his palms, sweeping them in front of him. "Why aren't you happy with just Sami and me?"

She had known he would say that. Tears were in her eyes as she reached for his hand. "I cannot explain it to you. It is all I want, all I can think of. I am supposed to have another child."

"You can't twist God's arm," Amir said, his warm hand encircling hers. "Creating life in a test tube. Bad things might happen. And Camille, I'm not up for this. Not now."

Camille laid her cheek on his hand, her face toward his, and he caressed her hair. "Will you think about it?"

"Of course, *motek*." He kissed the bridge of her nose. "We can think about it."

CHAPTER SIXTEEN

———— ··•◆•◆•·· ————

*C*amille parked in a downtown garage, behind the seafood restaurant Catch 35, and walked with brisk steps in the piercing cold to the fertility clinic. Sami was at nursery school for three hours, so since she hadn't needed Sabiha to watch her, she didn't have to lie about her plans. Camille stopped on the corner to turn off her location sharing from her iPhone. Amir could see on his Tesla phone app where Camille had parked, but she could be anywhere in the downtown shopping area. He had convinced her to get Charlie, so she would persuade him to make a baby.

She went inside the clinic, and her eyes adjusted to the dimmer light. New Age spa music played from the speakers in the waiting room. It had closed blinds; she assumed others were like herself, ashamed to need help for such a primary female function. Her thoughts were reaffirmed when she read the sign, "Privacy is assured," at the check-in counter. She was the only one in the waiting room and wondered if they staggered appointments. Had the 9:40 already entered?

A cheery young woman opened the glass divider at the reception desk, made a copy of her driver's license, and collected the three hundred and fifty dollars for the initial consultation fee. Camille paid in cash, not wanting Amir to see the bill on their shared credit card. The center did not accept health insurance, though its slogan was, "Planned and designed with the patient in mind." Camille deduced which patients they had in mind when they built this center in the town's wealthiest area. The price was inconsequential to her and likely to most infertile women in the suburb.

The reproductive endocrinologist, Dr. William Nett, welcomed her into his office. Multiple degrees and awards were mounted on the wall. He sat behind his desk, with his lab coat draped over the back of his chair like a superhero cape. His pale face was gentle and his voice soft; his mouth held a slight smile framed by his salt and pepper goatee. He seemed accustomed to the desperation Camille conveyed. He nodded as he listened to her experience, her trauma.

"And now, my sister, she is only twenty-eight, wants to be my surrogate." Camille's hands wrung the strap of her purse. "My husband, he is a doctor, too. He needs convincing."

Dr. Nett explained they would need to do an ultrasound to evaluate her ovaries and also examine her sister. "In order to complete the IVF procedure in your surrogate, eggs must be removed from your ovaries while you are under anesthesia. I retrieve eggs using a needle under ultrasound. The needle will remove all of the eggs which developed from both your ovaries."

"And will my sister need anesthesia to take the eggs?"

"She will not take the eggs, actually," Dr. Nett angled his computer screen toward her and showed her a black and white image of what resembled bubbles stuck together, like Sami's toy wand when she blew the solution into the air and delighted at the floating bubbles it produced. "She will receive the embryos, these contracted cells here," he pointed to the bubbles, "that our embryologists will have cultivated in an incubator with your egg and your husband's sperm, directly into her uterine cavity. It is not any more painful than a PAP smear." He continued to scroll through images and magnified an image of their lab.

Camille remained seated, bent forward at the waist to look closer at the screen. The incubator that would store her future baby was a white sterile box imprinted with bold blue letters; "COOK." The incubator was not a soft bed, as she had imagined. It was science fiction come alive. "Does that say *cook?* You will cook my baby?"

The doctor smiled. "It's the name of the company that makes the incubator."

"I see. Maybe I am over-reading things."

"Surrogacy's a big decision. I'm here to answer any questions you have, Mrs. Hadad."

"You said embryos." Camille's gaze remained on the incubator image. "How many will you put inside Viva? I want one baby."

"If we have three viable embryos, we will implant all three to increase the odds of success. Twin pregnancy occurs in thirty percent of IVF patients."

"What if you grow triplets? Or what if four babies, are how you say, *viable?*" She imagined her sister with a pregnant belly as large as four watermelons.

"We have the option of selective fetal reduction with potassium chloride if that occurs, though it happens infrequently."

"Potassium chloride? Like they inject on death row? You will kill my extra babies? That are growing inside of Viva?"

"Like I said, that's rare. Usually only one or two embryos implant."

She stood so fast her purse dropped to the floor. Not only was this man playing God, but he also deemed himself the executioner. Amir had been right. Bad things could happen. Very bad things.

Dr. Ness stood and retrieved the dropped bag. "We can insert only one embryo, if you prefer." He handed her the purse. "But that does diminish the success rate significantly."

"And the extra babies will just live in eternity in the cooking box?"

"We will keep them safe if you decide to implant again, in the future."

She put her hand up, her palm forming a stop, as if to push him physically away. She opened the office door and walked to the exit without looking back. Tears welled in her eyes as the clinic door shut, the final nail in the coffin of her fertility. She would never consider surrogacy again.

With this sudden clarity, a whisper of her inner self tucked deep inside her heart, emerged. She'd been mourning the loss of her unborn children instead of appreciating the gift of Sami. It was time to move forward, just the three of them, and embrace every moment of their only child's upbringing.

CHAPTER SEVENTEEN

············ · ◆ ◆ ◆ · ············

Three weeks on the medication, and Amir felt cured. Risperidone was working; it had completely silenced the voice. He didn't experience any of the side effects Ravi had warned him of. They'd met twice more without Camille, Amir insisting she didn't need to know, at least not now. He was feeling more like himself and the illness had been a minor blip on the radar of his life.

He listened to the local NPR radio station as he drove to work. "Chicago's having the coldest recorded day in over thirty-three years," the broadcaster said. "If you can stay home today, you should; we are in a deep freeze danger. Wind chills will be hazardously low at minus fifty-eight degrees." Amir believed him, shivering as he sprinted the short distance from his car in the garage to the hospital entrance. The air was so cold it hurt to breathe deeply. He wondered if his first med-exec meeting would be postponed.

He went to the lounge and found Jade making herself a Keurig coffee. He waited his turn and watched her look around the vacant room. "Any more episodes?" she said. Her voice was quiet. "Panic attacks?"

"Thankfully no. It was one and done."

"Glad to hear it." She took her coffee and stepped aside for him. "Have the Bustelo, it'll put hairs on your chest."

"Camille says I'm hairy enough." He laughed but put the yellow packet in the machine. Bustelo was his favorite as well. Miss Dee stocked it especially for him.

"What's the first item on your agenda today, Chairman Hadad? Residents?"

"Definitely residents. Once we begin training Northwestern's residents, we can begin a full call schedule. Provide service, at all hours." He didn't mention

Camille's after-hours bleeding, or how his department could have prevented her infertility. He assumed Jade knew.

"As long as they pay us for home call, you shouldn't get too much push back from the partners."

"It's always a game of cat and mouse. Who moved the cheese, right?" Amir said. "We need to get paid, but we need to save lives, regardless."

"Agreed." Jade sipped her coffee and ate a donut. "I'm off to read. Meet you in there?"

"My case checked in with same day despite the weather advisory." An entire city could shut down, but patients would still show for their elective cases. As he headed to pre-op his phone vibrated with a group text message from Liz Higbee: *The med-exec meeting has been cancelled.*

He chuckled to himself; only administrators were allowed to stay home.

·· ♦ ♦ ♦ ♦ ·

Camille and Sami stayed in their pajamas all day. With the winter weather advisory, even Sabiha remained in her retirement home. Charlie ran in the backyard to do his business and hurried back indoors, curling next to Camille on the couch as Sami played with his floppy ears. Camille relished every second of their mommy-and-daughter slumber party, as they'd coined their free day.

They drank hot chocolate with marshmallows and watched Disney movies and *Mr. Rogers' Neighborhood.* They built a fort in the living room with sheets and pillows, pretending to barricade themselves from the fierce wind slamming against the shutters. As Sami played with the train set Viva had bought her, Camille, eavesdropping from the kitchen as she made lunch, smiled as Sami whispered inside the fort. "Patrick used to build train tracks," Sami said. Charlie growled. "Patrick says it's only the wind, Charlie. Don't be scared."

When it was time for Sami to nap, Camille sang her a French lullaby. "*Une chanson douce...*" Sami clapped at the sound of her mother's singing voice, as she'd never heard it until now. Camille hadn't felt like singing since her traumatic surgery, and now surprised even herself. She'd missed singing. It had been such an integral part of her life before Sami's birth. In college, she'd had starring roles in *Guys and Dolls* and *The Sound of Music*. A critic from the *Chicago Tribune* had called her voice "angelic."

Three lullabies later, Sami fell asleep with Charlie curled at the foot of her bed. Camille sat next to them in the rocking chair and opened her laptop. Since her visit three weeks prior to Dr. Ness, her search engine no longer included the term *surrogacy*.

Viva had been disappointed, but Camille also registered relief in her sister's voice. "Camille, all I want is for you to be happy. If you will now be content with only our Sami, of course, I am too. And one day I will give her a cousin to play with."

When she told Amir, his entire body sank into hers, as he hugged her in a long embrace. He nuzzled her neck, gave her a tender kiss, and told her how much he loved her. They'd made love that night and slept curled together, her hands entwined in his, as they had in college.

Rocking in the chair, Camille searched for local theaters until she found an advertisement. A performance venue in North Central College, BrightSide Theater, was holding community amateur auditions for *Hello, Dolly!*. She recalled the venue. She and Amir had attended several shows and concerts there before Sami was born. Perhaps it was time to perform again. She watched Sami sleeping and imagined her daughter in the audience, standing in her seat cheering for her. There was a bright side indeed, and she was turning toward it.

She went to the crib in the corner of the room and began to dismantle it.

CHAPTER EIGHTEEN

⋯·✦✦✦·⋯

*C*amille walked onto the wooden theater floor, her confidence from her former starring roles returning with each step. She stood center stage in the intimate, two-hundred-and-fifty-seat thrust stage theater and gave a seductive smile into the bright light. "Camille Hadad," she said. "I am auditioning for the role of Irene Molloy." The part had the humor and songs she enjoyed, without the pressure of being the lead. She was too young anyway to play Dolly. She had dressed in a full skirt with high-heeled boots to embrace the role.

"Whenever you're ready, Camille." A disembodied voice came from the control booth. When she gave the nod, she heard "Cue music."

The instrumental sounds of "Ribbons Down My Back" began, and Camille sang. With every note, her voice was steady, unwavering. She imagined Sami and Amir watching in the front row and sang as if to them. When she finished, the spectators and others auditioning in the orchestra seats gave her a standing ovation.

A slight man with an overbite and a cigarette tucked behind his ear, emerged from the booth. He walked down the aisle, took the stairs on the side of the stage, and shook her hand. "Albert," he said. "I'm the director. And you're better than anyone I've directed before locally," he said and showed her a clipboard with the list of characters. He'd written her name next to Irene Molloy. "The part is yours for the taking; no callbacks needed."

In college, Camille was accustomed to the accolades and attention her voice and appearance received. However, it had been years since she'd sung publicly. She gave a bow to the audience and thanked Albert.

"I'll see you at rehearsal," she said, gathered her full skirt in her hand, and stepped off the stage. Her light was shining again. The feeling reminded her of her early years with Amir, how she'd felt upon her first sight of him. She'd been on the quad after rehearsal and this guy, his backpack slung over his shoulder, so confident and strong, had jogged to her and asked if she'd join him for coffee. Most men looked at her from afar, but this one, he was unique. Finding him as charming as he was handsome, as she'd laughed at his lame pickup lines, she agreed to go for coffee at the student center. Four days later they'd parted. He sent roses their first night apart, with a card. *"I've met the woman of my dreams, Amir."* Corny, but cute.

She got in her Tesla, eager to celebrate Valentine's Day dinner with that hunk of a husband. She flipped through the three Sentry Mode video alerts on the car display; two were of people admiring the car and peeking inside, and in the last clip, a man in a black overcoat appeared to lean in front of the vehicle, but his motion to and from the camera wasn't recorded. He appeared for two seconds and vanished from the screen. She tried to play the video again, but it was erased. A recording glitch, Camille assumed. She checked the back and front camera displays for any movements and drove.

She felt fortunate.

CHAPTER NINETEEN

········ • ◆ ◆ ◆ • ·········

*W*ith Camille in theater life, Amir's home was once again filled with music and gossip. After afternoon rehearsals they would have dinner, and Camille would put Sami to bed, then join him for a glass of wine on the couch. She'd chatter about her castmates, as she had in college, having grown particularly fond of Eva, the woman playing Dolly. "She is so funny, Amir. She has traveled the world with her husband; they never had any kids and preferred to stay child-free. Can you imagine? She calls it child-*free,* not child-*less.*"

Driving to work this morning, Amir reflected on how stressful seeing her depressed had been. Perhaps Ravi had been correct in his first visit that his hallucinations were part of a "fight or flight response" his mind created to deal with Camille's unhappiness. If so, perhaps he could taper off the risperidone.

At his reading station, with coffee in hand, he read three plain films. A wrist was next. He marked it on hold to get Jade's opinion; it had been a while since he'd read a wrist. He read the ICU chest X-rays next and magnified one. Using the hospital phone, he called the ICU physician. "You've got a pneumothorax in CV12; patient name Kirk. Looks like the central line is in good position, but someone dropped the lung in the process."

"My fellow just poked that one. Are you certain you want residents?"

Amir laughed. "It's not all bad, I hope."

"I'll put in a chest tube... appreciate the quick catch, Amir."

After he'd caught up on reads, he headed to the MRI suite. Bright yellow caution signs lined the walls along the hallway. At the entrance, he read "Caution MRI Zone III" with an image of a magnet with a lightning bolt through it. The vault handle, a long metal bar that reminded him of an old bank safe from the movies, was locked into position as the machine was active.

His afternoon patient was in the tube getting scanned in preparation for his kyphoplasty. Amir looked over the seated woman's shoulder, a petite, recent MRI technology graduate named Hannah. He studied the images she was taking.

"Sagittal T1?" Amir said.

"One more axial then ready for contrast," Hannah said. "I'll shoot it over to you in fifteen minutes."

"All right, tumor at T7 as expected." He pointed to a vertebra on her screen. "All that bone is now…" Amir's head involuntarily jerked to the right, and his jaw clenched. He tried to speak but couldn't.

Hannah looked at him. "You okay, Dr. Hadad?"

He knew what was happening—the risperidone side effect he'd most feared, tardive dyskinesia. He had no control over his clenched jaw and couldn't answer the tech. He went to a staff bathroom, locking the door behind him, and paced alone. He took calming breaths through his nose and rubbed his face. "No, no, no…" he thought. "This needs to stop… stop!" His heart rate increased. Once his clenched jaw finally released, he took a massive breath through his open mouth.

After a few more breaths, he looked in the mirror as he splashed cold water on his face. His eyes were bloodshot, and his mouth was dry. Someone knocked on the door.

"Dr. Hadad?" Hannah said. "Do you need assistance?"

"I'm okay. I'll be right out."

He rubbed his cheeks again and strode to the doctors' lounge to retrieve his coat. He returned to the bathroom, fumbling in his pockets until he found the medicine vial. He dumped the remaining risperidone pills into the toilet, and flushed. Ravi would have to prescribe him something safer.

CHAPTER TWENTY

— · · ✦ ◆ ✦ · · —

"I'm on my way home, now," Ravi said into his car speakerphone. He drove a leased 2019 Cadillac CT6 sedan, a luxury car he appreciated, especially in Chicago's long winter. The heated leather seat soothed his lower back as Ravi drove along snow-lined roads. He had just met with Amir, who was convinced he'd experienced tardive dyskinesia.

"Rav, do you want to eat at Ted Montana's?" Ali said. He could hear their sons laughing in the background, probably playing with their Lego sets.

"Sure, I'll drive if you want to start bundling the boys. It's too cold to walk."

Ravi turned the Sirius satellite radio to classic rock and pondered Amir's case. It was such an unusual presentation to have auditory and visual hallucinations, with no prior mental illness, at age thirty-eight. And to have tardive dyskinesia on such a low dose for only six weeks was not likely. Amir had probably experienced the restlessness seen with akathisia, not tardive dyskinesia as he'd claimed. Regardless, the side effects were troubling.

Since Amir was on such a low dose of Risperidone, Ravi didn't feel he needed to taper off, and he prescribed him Seroquel instead. If Seroquel was too sedating, Ravi would consult his colleagues on which medicine to try next. He needed to keep the hallucinations away, which risperidone had, without disabling Amir with side effects.

As he drove West on Ogden Avenue, his headlights flickered. His car radio short circuited and switched to a Christian music station; a pipe organ played. He fiddled with the audio, but was unable to turn it off. It played louder. He considered pulling into a gas station, but since the car's dashboard showed no alerts, he continued along. The organ music was pleasant. He matched the traffic's speed of forty miles an hour despite fresh snow on the streets.

As he turned left off Washington Street and onto Benton Avenue, the car's power failed—it stalled and then came to an abrupt stop. "What the hell?" His gaze went to the rearview mirror; there was a pick-up truck turning onto Benton Avenue, at far too fast a speed. He jabbed the ignition button, his foot on the brake. His car remained silent; all electrical components were dead, except the radio. The organ music was at a crescendo. He heard the truck screech to stop behind him as he tried to push open the door. It wouldn't unlock.

A sound of metal crushing as his driver rear-side was slammed by the truck.

The smell of something burning and a sharp pain in his chest as his car was propelled forward. It hit the lamppost of Central Park Road and flipped onto its side. He hung suspended by his seatbelt in front of Benton Avenue Apartments. The last thing he saw was the gazebo in Central Park and undulating smoke circling before him.

CHAPTER TWENTY-ONE

⸺ ⋯ ◆ ◆ ◆ ⋯ ⸺

The control room overlooking the interventional radiology lab was empty as the morning staff were performing a procedure. Amir watched through the leaded glass as Jade sterilely accessed her patient's abdomen. She pressed a footpad to speak into the control room.

"Amir, I'll be done with this gastrostomy tube in about fifteen minutes. Sorry for delaying your DVT."

He pressed the speaker button on the panel in front of him. "Not a problem. I have plenty of charting to do."

He walked down the hall to the reading room and sat at his station. He and Camille had watched a film, French with English subtitles, in the living room after dinner last night; she seemed to enjoy it, and he was content to zone out while stroking her hair. He'd had plenty of opportunities to tell her about the hallucinations and risperidone but decided not to burden her as she was beginning to recover.

Amir was dictating his third chest X-ray from the ICU when he heard the code alarm and a female dispatcher's voice on the ceiling speaker. "Code Emory House… Interventional Unit… Code Emory House Interventional Unit."

He jogged down the hallway and saw Jade's patient now struggling to breathe. The anesthesiologist, Dr. Jim West, his silver hair swept into a low ponytail and his stethoscope around his neck, was at the head of the table giving the patient oxygen with a mask. He must have been walking by when the code hit to assist so quickly.

"He's twenty-five, no allergies… I must've punctured an artery!" Jade said.

Dr. West ran the code. He gave orders to the response team—nurses, pharmacy staff, internal medicine doctors—that were now filing into the room.

"Call the OR STAT. We need an operating room, a general, and a vascular surgeon now. Tell them for an open ex-lap. I'll intubate."

"I'll get the art line," Amir said and hyperextended the patient's arm. He felt for a pulse in the patient's wrist; it was barely palpable. Lexi handed him a twenty-gauge arrow, and he threaded the guidewire into the artery once he saw the familiar bright red flashback in the chamber. Lexi secured it to the tubing and hooked it up to the monitor for Dr. West and the team to see the pulsatile waveform; the red ripples of blood moving inside the patient's arteries.

"Blood pressure 80/55," Jade said. "He's spiraling." She put her hand on the patient's ballooning abdomen. It looked pregnant. "He's distending with blood."

Dr. West continued to run the code, and within minutes, they had him intubated and lined up. They transferred the patient onto a stretcher and awaited permission to transport to the operating room.

"Dr. Ellis and the team are scrubbing," Lexi said, hanging up the phone. "We can roll to OR 6."

···◆◆◆···

Amir and Lexi watched from the control room as environmental services cleaned the lab; the flurry of the code had left hospital hazardous waste—blue drapes torn and bloodied, soiled surgical gloves and masks, suction canisters filled with blood—and they were on their second mopping of the floor.

"I've never seen that before. In Interventional, I mean," Lexi said, her manicured nails tapping on the keyboard. She was still charting the code, documenting the times it all occurred—for the peer reviewers and lawyers, likely the only ones who would read it.

"It's a rare risk. To perforate. Terrifying how fast things can turn." Amir said. It was unusual for any serious event to occur in interventional radiology. He couldn't recall the last code. Perhaps it was two years ago, and that was on a very ill patient. He understood Lexi; his nerves were a bit frayed, and it hadn't even been his case.

"If it's a possibility at all, shouldn't we always have an anesthesiologist present?" Lexi said. "I mean, I can't intubate and run a code, and I'm the person at the head of the bed. I've never felt so helpless."

"That's impractical. We have them down the hall if we need them. You saw how fast Dr. West and the code team arrived. You did well, too."

"If you say so." Lexi shook her head.

"Are you feeling up to do the next case? I can ask Miss Dee to find someone else to help." His patient was a sixty-year-old man with a disorder that was causing multiple blood clots. Last week, Amir had placed a filter to prevent a blood clot from entering the patient's lungs, and now would do a mechanical removal of the clot.

"Last time, he did great with minimal sedation. I can do it," Lexi said. "Just don't perf anything, okay?"

An hour later, the team had the patient loaded and ready. Amir put on his leaded apron and tucked his hair into a surgical cap and scrubbed. He pushed the door with his lower back to enter, holding his hands up for sterility. The tech, Mrs. Hunter, held the sterile gown open for him to slide his arms into, then she slipped a sterile size-eight glove onto each of his hands. She'd already prepped and draped the groin of the patient.

"Okay up there for me to begin?" Amir said.

"Stable and resting," Lexi said.

Amir injected lidocaine, creating a wheal on the skin, and then went a bit deeper. He continued with the thrombolysis, and at the very end, as he was sucking out the last of the clot, there was a power surge to the room; all the power failed—the lights, monitors, everything—and the generator did not kick in. Darkness enveloped the room.

"He isn't breathing! I can't feel a pulse!" Lexi said.

Amir ran into the hall and pressed a code button. He flipped the overhead light switch on and off until the room lit. "Give Epi!" Amir said as he began chest compressions.

The code team filled the room for the second time that day. They resuscitated for forty minutes before the anesthesiologist called it. Amir knew it was futile by the mottling, the blue veins of death all over his patient's ice-cold skin.

"Time of death… 11:56," Amir said.

Lesson number one.

He looked around, from Lexi to the code team to his dead patient on the table. There was something in the corner of the room—black, cold, smoke. He crept closer to the corner, heart thumping. The smoke passed through him and his body felt as though he'd been submerged in frigid water.

Bury me.

"Stop!" Amir yelled, holding his hands to his ears, crouched with his eyes squeezed shut. He was panting, heaving. He wanted to throw up. "Stop!"

When he opened his eyes again, the smoke had vanished—his colleagues were huddled around him, watching with bewildered concern and fear. Lexi came to his side, crouched by him, and whispered, "Dr. Hadad?"

CHAPTER TWENTY-TWO

A mir tore off his sterile gown and gloves and stumbled down the hall. He heard Lexi call out after him, but he left the code team and the dead body in the procedure room, grabbed his coat from the reading room, and hurried to the parking garage. The voice was laughing now, a continuous loop, enjoying his misery.

He peeled out of the parking garage and called Ravi. Ravi's call went to voice mail, and there was no answer at his office. He turned onto Ogden Street and sped into the office complex. He ran from the car into the complex and tugged at the office door entrance. It was locked. A note was taped on the window panel.

"Dear patients, the clinic will be closed indefinitely. We regret to inform you Dr. Ravi Patel was critically injured in a car accident yesterday. Please keep his family and staff in your prayers as we get through this difficult time."

The laughter in his head ceased, but the voice returned.

Lesson two.

· · ♦ ♦ ♦ · ·

"You aren't looking well," Sabiha said as she opened the door, ushering him in. She put her palm to his forehead. He caught a glance of himself in her foyer mirror. His eyes had bags under them and his thick raven hair, usually tamed by grooming products, looked as if he'd run his fingers through it for hours—which he had as he'd sat in the parking lot of Ravi's clinic, ignoring the repeated calls from the hospital and Camille. He turned his phone off after the tenth missed call notification.

"I have no one else to turn to, Savtah. Something awful's happening." His voice was hoarse.

"Are Sami and Camille okay? Your parents?"

"No. I mean, yeah. They're all fine."

"Come and sit." She helped him off with his coat and hung it on a hook under the mirror. "Let me turn the *koom-koom* on and make us some tea."

Amir sat at the kitchen bar stool with his head in his hands and elbows resting on the countertop as Sabiha put an electric kettle on. She poured the hot water over tea bags and added honey to his mug.

"Drink," she said, handing it to him. She led him to her living room couch and sat across from him. "Take a deep breath and start at the beginning."

Amir didn't realize how insane he sounded until he said the words aloud. "It's a man…" he began and told Sabiha every detail—the voice, the black smoke and organ music, the electrical outage, and now Ravi's car accident. "I think he killed two patients today. He definitely killed mine. He tried to kill Ravi." Amir began to weep. He felt like a four-year-old, running to his grandmother after falling from his bicycle.

Sabiha rose from her armchair and rummaged through her kitchen cabinet. She found a red velour jewelry satchel, the size to hold a ring, and filled a glass with tap water. She handed Amir the glass. "Hold this, *motek*."

She poured the contents of the satchel into the water. Silver droplets of mercury swirled in the glass. She took it from him and held it on top of his head, studying it. As if it were draining, the water began to spin, a spiraling effect, as the mercury formed a shape. She took her reading glasses from the top of her head, put them on, and moved closer to study the mercury.

"A noose," she said, her voice resolved. "The man who wants you to bury him was hanged." She took the glass from Amir's head and the water became still. "What does this man sound like?"

Amir was calmer now. He should've come to her from the start. He dried his tears with the sleeves of his shirt. "He's Irish. He sounds Irish."

Sabiha put her hand over her mouth. She grabbed his hand. "Now," she said. "We must go to your house, hurry."

···✦✦✦···

Amir drove the quarter mile as Sabiha sat in the passenger seat with her hands gripping the glass of water. The mercury had settled on the bottom of the glass in an amorphous shape, the noose gone. He took the glass from her as she used her walker to get out of the car and they entered through the kitchen. Charlie barked and ran to them, standing on his hind legs to lick at Amir's face. Amir gave the glass back to Sabiha.

Camille was at the kitchen counter with her phone to her ear, her eyes bloodshot as though she'd been crying. She put the phone down. "Where have you been? The hospital cannot find you and that Lexi called twice. You do not answer my calls. I was calling the police!"

Amir went to her, and buried his face in her neck. His arms enveloped her. "I'm so sorry," he said. "I couldn't call you. I'll tell you everything now."

"Why didn't you call me? You terrified me!" She said, crying. "We drove to the parking lot where your phone said you were, but you were not there! I was so scared."

"I can explain," he said.

Sami came from the living room and leaned her head against his leg. "Daddy!" He picked her up, the three of them embracing, as Sabiha waited at the kitchen counter.

"Sami," Sabiha said when Amir looked her way. "I need to ask you about your friend, Patrick."

CHAPTER TWENTY-THREE

· · ◆ ◆ ◆ · ·

*D*r. Liz Higbee went to her office in the administrative wing of the hospital, told her secretary, Olivia, she was "not to be disturbed," and locked the door behind her. Her fur coat hung on the coat rack, as did her Louis Vuitton tote. She sat at the expansive mahogany desk her predecessor left behind.

Something didn't add up. Amir had always seemed level-headed and in control; it was why she selected him as Chairman. She recalled how jittery he appeared that day in the doctor's cafeteria when she'd told him of the promotion. And now. His patient died on the table, and he had a "panic attack"? Why was he behaving differently?

She thought of her late husband. She had met William when he was a fifty-nine-year-old widow at a Healthcare Summit in Boston, and although he was fifteen years her senior, his vitality was of a fit and youthful man. His children were grown, and he didn't mind that she was peri-menopausal. He was wise, strong, and loving and not the least bit interested in having more children; he was ready to spoil a wife, and that he did. They'd married and lived sixteen joyful years together until the disease arrived.

He fought the lymphoma with chemo and radiation like the warrior he was, and at one point, appeared to be in remission. Then one night, she'd found him passed out in the bathroom of their home.

When the end was inevitable, William's doctor had been so kind to her, so patient, explaining William's altered mental state, poor prognosis, and the need for hospice. He hadn't run out of the hospital in a panic attack!

She typed *Amir Hadad Deceased Patients* into her secure computer and read the pre-op that Amir had completed on his electrocuted patient hours earlier. She flagged it and composed an email to the medical executive president.

"Please follow and review this case. I am concerned Dr. Hadad's mental health contributed to this patient's demise. He fled the hospital without meeting with the patient's family, and his partner and nurse covered for him. I suspect drug abuse."

· · ✦ ✦ ◆ ✦ ✦ · ·

Sabiha held Sami on her lap while Amir and Camille sat on the couch. The fading sunlight hit the ice crystals on the front yard's oak tree, and the reflections it created danced through the storm windows. Nature's disco ball, Camille called it once.

"Sami. Your friend Patrick," Sabiha said, cuddling her great-grandchild. "What's he like?"

"He's funny." Sami held her doll and brushed its golden hair.

"How so?"

"He calls me Johanna."

"Do you know Patrick's last name?"

Sami looked at the recliner in corner of the room and appeared to hear something. "Doyle. He says Doyle."

"He's with us?" Sabiha followed Sami's gaze to the upholstered recliner. The cushions of the seat rose as though a person had risen from it; just barely perceptible.

"He just left," Sami said, while wriggling out of Sabiha's lap. "Savtah you squeezing me. Too much."

Camille joined Sami on the rug in front of the fireplace. She stroked her child's cheek. "I heard you tell Charlie that Patrick worked on the railroads. Do you know where he worked, baby?"

"He works near us."

Amir and Sabiha shared a glance and went to the kitchen, leaving Camille and Sami in the living room. They spoke in Hebrew with soft voices.

"A hanged Irishman named Doyle. We must find where his remains are …"

"And bury the bastard," Amir said. "*I'll* bury the bastard. But first I'm getting my family the hell out of here."

· · ✦ ✦ ◆ ✦ ✦ · ·

It took convincing to get Camille to take Sami and stay with her mother in Paris.

"And what about the play? I made a commitment," Camille said. "There is ethics in theater, and you do not abandon your cast."

"We have no choice. Doyle's killing people! You have to go."

"I do not have to go. I can stay and help. Nothing you are saying is making any sense."

"Camille, he has attached to Sami." Amir sat next to her on their bed and put his arm around her, pulling her close. "We must protect her."

Camille dropped her head and squeezed the bridge of her nose while she considered his words. "Sami sees a ghost? And he killed your patient?" She whispered. "Maybe there is another explanation?"

"I know it's difficult to believe, *motek,* but I need you to trust me and leave with Sami."

Camille pulled away and shook her head.

"It's temporary. Camille, please." Amir took her hands in his. "I'm begging you to go."

"You have one week," she said. "Then we are coming home."

She pulled out her cell phone. "I need to tell Albert," she said.

Amir listened while she apologized for missing upcoming rehearsals. She said she didn't know when she'd return. "There is a family emergency in France," she said over speakerphone.

"I'll have your understudy prepare," Albert said, "but the part's still yours when you return. I pray for good news for your family."

When she hung up, Amir hugged her and said, "Thank you."

"One week," she said, kissing his cheek. "That is all."

Amir wanted Sabiha to flee as well and go to his parents and brother in Israel, but she refused, speaking in Hebrew to him. "I'm staying with you, *motek.* Patrick Doyle knows I want to help him. He won't hurt me."

CHAPTER TWENTY-FOUR

···•◆•◆•◆•···

hile Camille packed, Amir booked airline tickets and Sabiha worked in Amir's office. She searched "Patrick + Doyle + Hanging." She found a website, "Living History of Illinois," and there on page seventy-four of "The History of the County of DuPage Illinois," was Doyle's story. She called out to Amir and with fear pointed to the computer screen. Amir read aloud over her shoulder.

DuPage Observer

Naperville, Illinois

October 26, 1853

On Monday of last week a most revolting murder was committed on the line of the Chicago, St. Charles and Mississippi Air Line Railroad, in this county. The particulars, so far as we have been able to learn them, are as follows: Two brothers, Irishmen, named Tole, who had been employed upon the road, had received their pay in the morning, amounting to sixty dollars and had quit work.

They were indulging in a little 'spree,' and one of them became very drunk. An Irishman named Doyle, by some means knew of the money in their possession, and it is supposed determined upon robbing them.

He found an opportunity to make the attempt the same afternoon. It seems all three were traveling together on the

St. Charles and Chicago wagon road, and when near the residence of Mr. Clisby, one of the brothers Tole became so stupid from the effects of liquor as to be unable to proceed further; in other words, he was dead drunk, and fell off the wagon onto a fence corner.

The sober brother stopped to move him, and assist him to proceed, and while thus engaged over him, Doyle, it would seem, conceived the fitting moment to have arrived. Doyle proceeded to the fence, gathered a fence stake, and returning to the two brothers struck the sober one over the head, and continued to beat him until he was senseless, literally knocking out his brains. He then rifled the pockets of his victim and drunken companion, and went on a short distance, to a house, where he got something to eat.

The bloodied pocket book, which contained the money, was found a few rods distance from the murdered man, in the direction of the house where Patrick Doyle stopped to eat. Doyle then went down to Warren station, but not meeting the cars, proceeded to the Junction, where he took the Aurora train for Chicago.

Justice moved swiftly! He was immediately pursued to the city, information and a description of the person telegraphed to Chicago, and on Thursday afternoon, deputy sheriff S.E. Bradley arrested him as he was walking on Randolph Street. Sheriff T.W. Smith started early on Friday morning and brought the prisoner back to Naperville about noon of the same day. The grand jury had not yet adjourned at the county courthouse, and an indictment was found against him that very day!

In the late afternoon he was brought into court, which was still in session, and presented with a copy of the indictment. Having no counsel, the court assigned him two prominent Naperville attorneys to defend him; R.N. Murry

Esq., who had served as sheriff and school commissioner, and Nathan Allen Esq., a former probate justice and county judge. After consultation with the State's attorney, it was agreed to allow the prisoner to plead to the indictment at the next term of the circuit court. He was committed to the courthouse jail, his cell overlooking the Town Square, to await his trial.

Coroner F.W. Hagemann held an inquest over the body of the murdered man, and the verdict of the jury was that he came to his death by "being willfully murdered at the hands of Patrick Doyle."

The name of the deceased was Patrick Tole and he is about 25 years of age. There does not appear to have been any feud or quarrel existing between the Tole brothers and Doyle, whatsoever, nor do they appear to have been in any sort of affray at the time the crime was committed, which makes the case look still more aggravated.

The trial was brief! And on Friday, May 12 of this year, Patrick Doyle, 24, a thin, spare man, swung at the end of a rope below a giant oak at the bottom of the hill, southside of Chicago Avenue across from Huffman Street.

It was a gala occasion and as many of DuPage county's 5,609 residents attended as possible.

"He was executed by hanging ... 'swung at the end of a rope below a giant oak at the bottom of the hill, southside of Chicago Avenue across from Huffman Street!' Amir, he was hanged right between our homes! Maybe that's why he's haunting you?"

"He told me, but I thought I was psychotic." Amir rubbed his chin, reading through the entire chapter. "1853. How the hell will there still be remains to bury?"

"Maybe they were preserved? We need expert help; this is all I could find on the internet."

"An archivist. Tomorrow after I take Camille and Sami to the airport, we'll find an archivist."

· · ◆ ◆ ◆ ◆ · ·

When Amir returned upstairs to help Camille pack, Sabiha went to their garage and unlocked Camille's car. She opened the passenger side door and fumbled in Sami's car seat until she found it. She held the *sha-sha*, the gold amulet to ward off spirits, and called up the stairs, "Samira, come."

Sami came down the stairs in her lopsided gait, with the doll still in her hands, and Sabiha gathered her in her arms. "I have something very special… your first gold necklace, *motek*. I want you to wear it always." She hung the necklace on Sami, and it lay across her belly. Sami smiled, admiring it. "It's older than I am. Treat it with the love you treat me."

She glanced upstairs at Camille's watchful gaze, and said, "Is it okay, Camille?"

"She will never take it off, Sabiha. I promise."

CHAPTER TWENTY-FIVE

······◆·◆·◆··· ─

*I*n the morning, Amir drove Camille and Sami to O'Hare. He helped them check in. The whole time Sami clung to his neck, unconvinced this was a "fun mommy-daughter vacation." He snuggled her as her legs wrapped tightly around his torso, and she wailed. "Daddy and Charlie come too."

"We can't, my little one. You give Mamé Renée a lot of love. She's so excited you're coming." He kissed her cheeks, which were wet with tears. "You know they have the most delicious cakes in France?"

"Cake?" She stopped crying and pulled away from his neck. "What cake?"

"Oh, little doll, *ma poupée,* so many kinds!" Camille took her from Amir, preparing to go through security. "Crème Brûlée, Éclairs, macarons! We can bring macarons home to Daddy and Savtah."

Camille kissed Amir goodbye at security. "Text me all the time, *mon amour.* I do not care the time difference."

"I will." He held his family in a tight embrace, giving each of his girls another kiss and inhaling their scent. He was going to eradicate this furious, cruel spirit from their lives.

··· ◆ ◆ ◆ ·· ·

Amir's heart was heavy as he entered the hospital. He took the elevator to the ICU. Miss Dee had removed him from the schedule for two weeks on sick leave, and he'd texted Jade and Lexi an apology; they both had managed the initial ramifications of his patient loss, talking with the family and the pathologist after he'd fled. Jade explained he'd experienced a severe panic attack and did her best to smooth things over with the hospital staff and administration, specifically Liz

Higbee. Amir let her believe that was the case. He didn't want Doyle to target her next.

Amir found Ravi's room on the fourth-floor intensive care unit. His friend was sitting in bed, eating lunch a woman with long raven hair fed him. Ravi's forehead had a dressing over it, his face was bruised, and his right arm was in a cast.

"Amir, come, come," Ravi said.

The woman turned to him in an abrupt motion, and he recognized Ravi's wife, Ali. She hadn't changed much since they were in medical school. "Amir?" Ali said, studying his face. She stepped back. "Amir with the *bhoot?*"

"A *bhoot?*" Amir said. He remained at the door, unsure if Ali wanted him there.

"You have a ghost, no? Something evil?"

"How did you know that I have a ghost?"

"Ravi's car was hijacked by your *bhoot.* He tried to kill him."

"Ali. We don't know it was a ghost. It could have been an electrical failure." Ravi pulled her close to him, stroking her hand.

"Ali's right," Amir said. "His name's Patrick Doyle, and he used to work on the railroads. I believe he was hanged here in Naperville in 1853 and needs me to bury him."

Ali crossed her arms as he spoke and said, "I knew it."

"He can short circuit electronics." He told them about the electrical outage and his patient death the day before. He updated Ali on all the auditory hallucinations he now believed had been Doyle speaking to him. "He will continue to harm others until I find his remains and bury them."

Ali walked to her purse and pulled out her phone. "I will help you find him," Ali said. "What's your number? I'll text you mine."

"Ali, if it's a *bhoot,* I don't want you involved!" Ravi's voice was hoarse, and Amir figured it was due to the breathing tube for the surgery. "Absolutely not."

She went to his bedside and whispered in his ear. He closed his eyes and finally gave a nod. "We will find the remains of this tortured soul," Ali said to Amir. "To protect you and my family, we must."

· · + ♦ ♦ + · ·

Amir stopped at Dr. Higbee's office on the first floor. He knocked on the door as her secretary was away. "Come in," he heard her familiar deep voice.

"Amir, how're you feeling?" She stood and motioned to the chair in front of her desk. "Please."

"I'd like to apologize for my erratic behavior yesterday." Amir took the offered seat but left his coat on. He noticed a framed picture of Liz and an older man and recalled she was a recent widow. "I can't explain what happened to me, but my behavior was unacceptable."

"Jade said you're suffering from panic attacks?" She leaned forward in her desk.

"I'm seeking therapy for it."

"And we're supporting you." She reached into her desk and wrote on a pad. "Here's the number of a talented behavioral therapist I know. She specializes in the treatment of all anxiety disorders."

Amir took the paper; "From the Desk of Dr. Elizabeth Higbee" was in bold type on the bottom. "Thank you. For this, and the support."

"Amir, unfortunately, I will need you to go down the hall to the lab now, and give a urine sample."

"What?"

"The medical executive president said it's standard procedure if a physician is suspected of drug abuse."

"You just said you're supporting me. And now you don't believe me?"

"If it was a panic attack, you have nothing to hide, right?" Liz leaned forward and lowered her voice. "I need to protect the patients of this community, Amir. Please understand this is protocol."

"Yeah, fine. I'll give a sample. Thanks so much for *understanding*."

She gave him a closed-lipped smile as he stood. "Please stop by the morgue as well, and speak with the forensic pathologist. She emailed me earlier; she can't conclude the autopsy investigation of your patient without your statement. The funeral home's waiting for her to release the body."

Amir was conflicted with anger at Liz and guilt for his patient. He'd been so consumed with protecting his own he hadn't thought enough of his patient's family. He would call them and apologize for not speaking with them sooner. He gave the urine sample as instructed and took the stairs to the basement, where he found Dr. Petra Warne performing an autopsy on a woman who appeared to have been pregnant.

Dr. Warne, dressed in scrubs with her short spiked hair contained in a surgical cap and her back turned to him, had cut the cadaver from neck to pubis and was speaking to herself as she examined the internal organs. "The uterus is enlarged, I'll cut that last," she said to no one.

As he got closer, the smell made him nauseous. He'd never understood how the pathologists tolerated it. The only time he had witnessed an autopsy was in medical school—the patient was a seven-year-old boy who'd been shot in the head as his baby brother played with their father's shotgun. He realized that day he could never specialize in pathology, or pediatrics, for that matter. Dead children were not something he would be able to compartmentalize and cope with.

"You get by the body and don't leave it," Dr. Warne said, watching him struggle to breathe. "Your olfactory system adapts and the smell becomes obsolete. But if you want, there's peppermint oil on the counter. To put under your nose."

He stood close to the body hoping his nose would adapt quickly, already well aware the peppermint oil didn't mask the smell. It only made him despise peppermints.

"Did you determine my patient's cause of death?" Amir asked.

"Cardiac arrest from Vfib. The amount of current that passed through his body must've been over 200 milliamps." She'd previously cut the skull with a bone drill and dissected the pregnant woman's brain. Now she extracted it, and holding it in her gloved hands, turned to weigh it on the scale behind her.

"But he was grounded." Amir had seen Lexi put the blue grounding pad on the patient's thigh before they'd draped.

"He was. He had an enormous burn mark on his right upper thigh from it. Didn't matter, the current was strong enough. He died by electrocution and bad luck. This lady's luck was bad too… a hemorrhagic stroke." She pointed to the side of the brain; instead of yellowish-white, it was blackened from old blood.

The smell had abated, but Amir was eager to leave. "I'll fill out my statement and place it on your desk," he said. "I apologize for the delay."

She nodded, but her gaze was on the knife she was applying to the brain; he assumed she was preparing slices to study further. As he shut the door silently behind him, Doyle's voice returned.

You doctors sliced me from top to toe.

"I'll help you," Amir said, aloud and alone in the stairwell. "I'll help you as long as you don't hurt anyone else."

The voice was silent.

CHAPTER TWENTY-SIX

· · ✦ ✦ ✦ · ·

The Air France business class compartment was fully seated and the flight attendants passed through the aisle. The one wearing a single dolphin earring, with a name tag that read "Juliette," offered Camille a mimosa. It tasted expensive, and she sipped it while rocking Sami on her lap. Music with French lyrics played as passengers stored their carry-ons in the overhead bins. A businessman, across the aisle, was watching her. She gave him the look she used to deter any advances—Viva called it her "No chance in hell look." The man's gaze returned to his opened laptop and he put in earbuds.

The flight was behind schedule, and Camille sensed the crew's frustration with the slow response of some passengers to take their seats. "Welcome to Air France. My name's Karen, and I am your flight leader; safety is our top priority, and we are happy to serve you. We are past our departure time," Karen spoke into the speakerphone. "Please take your seats, and thank you for flying Air France." Karen repeated the message in French. Camille and Sami shared a singular seat pod and Camille lowered their window shade to better view the Disney movie *Mary Poppins Returns* on their personal display; Amir had given her a splitter to allow two sets of earphones to be plugged into the outlet since she and Sami were sharing a screen.

"Flight attendants prepare for departure and all call," Karen said.

As they taxied for liftoff, the airline safety video played, interrupting their movie. "Hey!" Sami said. Camille, however, was grateful to hear the tongue of her beloved country spoken. She did love France, despite her complicated relationship with her only remaining relative there.

Renée Block Barnard had raised her daughters in a perfunctory and superficial manner; appearance over substance. As a young girl, Camille had wondered if her mother would've loved her and Viva if they'd been unattractive. She dressed them like dolls, and rarely spoke to them on any deep level. When their father had died of a sudden heart attack when she was sixteen years old, her mother was of little comfort. It was Camille who consoled her baby sister Viva, sleeping in her bed as the girl wept. Renée had not shed a tear at the funeral, but she'd been impeccably dressed in Dior, told Camille not to slouch, and hid her eyes and emotions behind sunglasses and lipstick.

Amir's upbringing was so unlike hers, and Camille relished the Hadad family's physical and constant show of love. Occasionally, she was jealous of their closeness. Amir had turned to Sabiha when he was in need and not to her. It festered into anger as she considered it. Did he think she was too fragile to be trusted? Why hadn't he told her weeks ago when he first heard the voice? She'd said nothing of it last night or this morning, as she didn't want to cause him more distress.

She reclined her chair further, bringing the foot of the chair up, and Sami snuggled into her while her gaze remained on Mary Poppins, landing on a rooftop with an umbrella. Camille covered them with Sami's favorite blanket, an ultra-soft cotton and polyester blend Viva had given her on Sami's first birthday—it had white sheep and clouds on a blue background. Sami loved it so much, Viva had even bought Camille a spare she kept in Sami's bedroom closet, just in case it ever got lost.

She tucked Sami closer to her and wished they were headed to New York City to stay with Viva. Amir had insisted she leave the country, so she did as he wanted, pacifying him and Sabiha with this transatlantic flight. She fell asleep until the flight attendants began meal service.

As she was offered another cocktail from Juliette, the lights on the plane flickered. Sami looked to the aisle and said, "Patrick, not now. I'm watching a movie."

Doyle was real.

Camille caressed Sami's *sha-sha* necklace. She kept the Chamtzah, the hand of God, between her index finger and thumb. She'd never believed in such superstitious symbolism before, but until yesterday, she hadn't believed in ghosts, either. The plane hit a bump of turbulence, and the seatbelt sign came on. The captain interrupted Sami's movie again, speaking in French followed by English.

"Ladies and gentlemen, we're experiencing some minor turbulence. Please take your seats and fasten your…" The plane's nose lurched downward. The food carts veered to the front and pinned Juliette against the flight attendant seating, and the man with the laptop shrieked, "Jesus!"

"Oh God, oh God," Camille whispered, clutching Sami and the *sha-sha* to her chest. "Sami, ask Patrick to leave!"

Sami began to cry. "Momma!"

"Tell him to leave!"

"Patrick, go away!"

The man across the aisle was crying now, and she heard passengers scream, but as fast as it happened, it ended. The plane leveled, and the turbulence passed; the familiar feel of flight vibrated on the soles of her feet, and the plane's white noise silenced the cabin. She heard the woman behind her praying aloud, and after a few minutes, the captain's voice returned. "I apologize, ladies and gentlemen. I have full command of the craft; airspeed and altitude are fully restored. We were momentarily stalled due to a strong wind current, but we are well past it now. The New York Oceanic Sector has permitted us to proceed to Paris."

"You are sure Patrick left, baby?" Camille whispered.

"He was joking." Sami focused her attention on the end of her movie and leaned her head onto her mother's shoulder. "He went home." She flicked her hand, her palm facing up. It reminded Camille of a gesture Sabiha did, and she smiled through the tears. She stroked the fine baby hair of her only child and prayed for their safety. When the jet landed in Paris, the passengers, including Camille, applauded. Sami was asleep.

CHAPTER TWENTY-SEVEN

······◆◆◆······

*S*abiha was waiting with Charlie in the Sunrise Community circular drive, standing with her walker under the attached carport. Amir hopped out and opened the passenger door for her, folding her walker into the backseat.

"I'm so glad you stayed with me, Savtah." He started the car, and before putting it in drive, he checked the flight status of Air France on his smartphone. Camille wasn't using the plane's Wi-Fi to update him, and he assumed it wasn't working. The app showed their plane was somewhere over the Atlantic, with two more hours of flight. Perhaps Renée had mellowed a bit with age, and Sami could melt anyone's heart.

When they dropped Charlie at doggy daycare he ran in with his tail wagging. They drove to Naperville's renowned public library, The Nichols Library. Like most essential locations, it was named after a founding settler. Amir helped Sabiha out of the car at the entrance and found parking by an eight-foot-tall bronze sculpture of *The Cat in the Hat* in honor of Dr. Seuss. He smiled, thinking of Sami and how she adored that statue.

He and Sabiha located a librarian at the information desk. "We need as much information as possible on the execution of Patrick Doyle," Amir said.

"Oooh, what an intriguing request," the librarian said. "Let me check with Hannah; she's one of our archivists."

Sabiha and Amir waited in the "Quiet Zone"; several college students were whispering with open textbooks and computers on their shared table. A woman with Nordic features, her platinum blonde hair pulled into a tight ponytail, approached them.

"Were you looking for an archivist?" Hannah said. "How may I be of assistance?"

Amir had printed the webpage Sabiha found the night before and handed it to Hannah, explaining the request again. He had decided not to divulge any other information to protect Hannah from Doyle's wrath.

Hannah read over the details. "May 12, 1853. Wow, that does require some digging." She smiled. "Have you tried the Naper Settlement Museum? I imagine they have records in their historical catalog."

··◆◆◆◆··

The museum was within walking distance, but Amir drove, not wanting Sabiha to get fatigued. It stood on thirteen acres, an "open-air" museum, with restored homes and shops from when their city was the unincorporated Naper Settlement. Some of the Victorian homes from those early settlers remained intact throughout downtown as well, and the city took pride in its rich heritage. He read the sign at the museum entrance:

Established in 1969, this museum operates under the direction and governance of the Naperville Heritage Society, whose mission is to document, preserve, and interpret the community life of Naperville, Illinois, including, but not limited to the social, political, and business history.

Amir wondered if the legal hanging those early settlers had performed would be documented. He'd never heard of Patrick Doyle's execution before yesterday, but the museum's archivist, a man named Mark, wearing a Gay Pride shirt with a rainbow across the chest, certainly had.

"We get questions about Doyle all the time," Mark said. "I have a few articles I can show you… Wait here, they're in the archival storage."

Amir watched as a grade school class filed past them on a field trip. He heard the tour leader describe the museum's blacksmith shop. "You can take pictures and videos, kids, but don't touch anything. The forge is over 400 degrees Fahrenheit to heat the metal. You will see…"

Mark returned and said, "Pretty gruesome stuff." He handed Amir the original newspaper pages preserved in plastic sleeves. "All in the name of science, I suppose."

Amir and Sabiha sat next to each other in the reading room by the entrance, with the article they'd read online and four new ones they hadn't seen. Amir read the news clippings aloud. Mark hovered behind them, and Amir assumed he was protective of the historical documents.

The Belvidere Standard

Belvidere, Illinois

16 May, 1854, Tuesday

HUNG– Patrick Doyle was hung on the 12th at Naperville, for killing Patrick Tole last fall on the St. Charles Air Line Road. His demeanor upon the scaffold was most disgusting, cursing the officials and the audience, and swearing if they would untie his hands "he could whip any three men in the crowd." He was evidently a hardened wretch.

The Elgin Palladium

June 3, 1854

DISGRACEFUL BODY SNATCHING!

The following horrid transactions occurred over the corpse of Patrick Doyle, the murderer, who was recently hung at Naperville, DuPage Co., Ill. Such scenes awaken a disgust for the practice of dissection, whereas, if that practice were legalized, as it should be, they would never have been recorded:

"After his execution, a most disgraceful scene took place between certain physicians and others, in relation to the body of the murderer. After the execution, the body was delivered to the sexton, under his solemn and repeated agreement to bury it properly.

He proceeded with a physician and his student to the burying ground, where a grave had been previously dug, and lowered the coffin into it, and then he pretended to have business off at a distance from the grave.

While he was gone, the others unscrewed the coffin, took out the body, and hid it in the corner of the fence, and went away, and the sexton buried the empty coffin.

During this transaction, another physician and some others were watching them, and as soon as the first set of hyenas left, they stole the body from the place where the first set of thieves had put it, and hid it again in the woods.

The first party coming back and finding their booty gone, very naturally concluded that the body was in the woods nearby and laid in watch. As soon as it was dark, as was anticipated, the second gang came with their wagon to take the body away; then ensued such a scene that was probably never before witnessed: two gangs of robbers, calling themselves men, quarreling and gnashing their teeth over a dead body, to which neither had any right whatever, but which, by all the laws of the land, justice and decency, they were forbidden to touch in the first place.

It is said that knives and pistols were drawn, and threats made, but they did not go so far as to use them; and then the disgraceful row was ended by the first party buying the pretended right of the other, and taking the body to Naperville."

CLARION

June 4, 1931

Lewis M Rich, then 86, relates the following story:

"I must tell you about Patrick Doyle, the man who was hung... He was a prisoner in the Court House here awaiting his time for execution. My mother and her sister went to the jail, in the basement of the courthouse, to visit him. They talked and prayed with him and he seemed quite penitent... In a short time afterwards he was hung... His body was taken to the cemetery but stolen at night ... and taken about Swartz and Harding blacksmith shop (northwest corner of Washington and Water), and dissected the next noon. I climbed up a ladder and saw the body on a table. After dissecting him, they kept the bones, put the rest of the remains in a barrel, and put the barrel in Dr. Jassoy's barn.... When the flood came on Valentines' Day, three years later, the barn and barrel sailed down the river. But Doyle's skeleton remained, displayed in Dr. Hamilton Daniels' shop."

"Doctors stole his body! He was never buried, Savtah. What he's been telling me is true. They dissected him and left his remains in a *barrel?*"

"*Mesken,* the poor man," Sabiha shook her head. "No one should be treated with such disrespect in death. Even a murderer."

"*But the skeleton remained...* Where is it now?" Amir said.

"Keep reading," Mark said.

CLARION

April 5, 1923

"...and finally the hanged man was brought to light in the shape of a skeleton, which was kept for a long time in a room of Dr. Hamilton Daniels' drugstore, (located in the CLARION building), and when he retired from business, he donated it to the North Western College (now North Central) to demonstrate anatomy."

"So we go to North Central?" Amir said, with a glance at Mark. "They must have it."

"North Central has no recollection or any evidence of the bones. Their archivist believes it went to Chicago and not to them. In my extensive research, the paper trail stops with Dr. Daniels keeping it in his drugstore and then it vanished to a school that won't claim it."

"May I take a photo of these?" Amir said.

"No flash, those are delicate," Mark said. "I can Xerox you copies to take, as well."

As he took the photographs his phone vibrated, startling him.

Landed. Be safe!!! DOYLE WAS ON THE PLANE!

Amir's heart raced as his fingers typed.

WHAT?!?

We are fine, he left after scaring me to death. I believe you! I will call you in a few minutes. Taxiing to the gate.

Amir showed the message to Sabiha. She gasped.

"Amir, we must hurry!"

CHAPTER TWENTY-EIGHT

· · ◆ ◆ · ·

*J*uliette held a sleeping Sami, rocking her in her arms and humming a French lullaby. Camille gathered their belongings, opened the stroller, and reached for her child. "She's such a beautiful girl," Juliette said in French. "Welcome back."

As Camille buckled Sami into the stroller, the child didn't wake. It was five in the morning in Paris, and she hoped Sami might wake in a few hours to avoid jet lag. She cleared customs in the line for foreign nationals—Camille was a dual citizen of France and the United States, but Sami's passport was American—and took the elevator to baggage claim. Before collecting her luggage, Camille freshened up in the ladies' room. She changed out of her jeans and sweater and put on a dress her mother had sent a year ago. She tore the tags off with her teeth and put the black sheath with the fitted waist on, securing the leather belt and zipping the side closure. Her kitten heels completed the Renée-approved style.

She shoved the worn clothes inside her carry-on. With teeth brushed, lip gloss applied, and her sandy blonde hair brushed and pinned, she collected her suitcase and rolled it and Sami's stroller into Roissy's Arrivals Hall. It didn't take long to locate her mother at the usual spot sitting at Frenchy's Bistro sipping coffee; her mother was punctual, predictable, and placid. Dressed in tailored slacks, her trademark sunglasses perched atop her head, Renée was reading the newspaper. Sabiha would be watching for them, standing and excited to greet them, but Renée was waiting for them to find her, despite this being her first time to meet Sami in person. Camille felt a rise of anger, and her mother hadn't even spoken yet.

Camille continued walking, out of Renée's line of vision, and called Amir. After reassuring him Doyle had disappeared and would likely not bother her again, it was his turn to calm her. "It should just be a few days with your mom," he told her. "Sabiha and I are going to find Doyle and you two can come home. And Camille, you could use this time to finally talk about what happened, in person." His voice was as comforting as her father's had been. How she missed her dad, her Papa, and wished she was visiting with him, instead.

She turned and went to the bistro, keeping the stroller in front of her as a shield. "Maman," Camille said, and as her mother looked at her, Camille was glad she'd changed clothes. The look was one of satisfaction, since her doll, her daughter, was dressed to her liking. Renée stood and gave Camille a kiss on each cheek. She smelled of rose perfume, the same brand Camille knew as a child.

"Darling, how lovely you are," Renée said and then bent to examine her sleeping granddaughter. Her hand reached for the *sha-sha*. "What's this tacky jewelry the child's wearing?"

Camille took a deep breath and hoped Amir would find Patrick Doyle quickly.

CHAPTER TWENTY-NINE

"*A*nd Camille, you could use this time to finally talk about what happened, in person," Amir said, whispering in the lobby of the museum. He was saddened to hear Camille's frustration with her mother, hoping they could find resolution if Camille was persistent enough. He reassured her that everything would be okay, and to give her mother a chance. "Please text me pictures, I miss you."

Moments later Camille sent a selfie. She had changed into a dress and was crouched by Sami, who was asleep in her stroller. God, how he loved them.

Amir called to update Ali. "Now we know why Doyle's targeting doctors. He has a justified vengeance," Ali said. "I teach in the Biology Department and have many connections. I'll start with an archivist I know, Vejin. Maybe she can probe further than the museum could."

"How's Ravi?" Amir said.

"Neurosurgery signed off, so he's out of the ICU. Hoping we get to go home tomorrow."

"Meet you there?"

"Oesterle Library. It's open only to students and faculty, so I'll ask Vejin to let you in. Let me text her now. I'm waiting for Ravi's mother to come visit in the hospital. When she gets here I'll come. I don't want to leave him alone."

· · + ◆ ◆ + · ·

A striking woman with high cheekbones and full lips, wearing a hijab, opened the library door. "Please, come in. I hear we're digging for actual bones!"

Amir introduced himself and Sabiha.

"My grandmother's name is Sabiha. Where are you from?"

"Iraq," Sabiha said and flipped her speech to Arabic. "Do you speak Arabic?"

"We're from Kurdistan. *Tasharrafna!* It's an honor to meet you," Vejin responded in Arabic.

She led them to her office at a slow pace to accommodate Sabiha.

"The Kurds and the Iraqi Jews, we share so much in our struggles to exist in peace," Sabiha said. "Do you have family there?"

"My cousins and grandparents are still there. Everyone is well."

"*Ma sha Allah*," Sabiha said. "What God wishes, may they stay safe."

They took the elevator to the second floor past the computer lab. Student art work was displayed along the hall leading to Vejin's office. She offered Sabiha a seat next to her at her desk and Amir stood, looking over Vejin's shoulder as she typed "Doyle + Skeleton" into CardinalSearch, the college's internal search engine.

"This is a brand-new search engine for us; perhaps it can find what others couldn't."

Moments later two articles appeared on her screen. "*Hasanan!* Found it! His skeleton was here, that's for certain. I'll print these for you," Vejin said and then read aloud the articles on the screen.

THE COLLEGE CHRONICLE OF NORTH CENTRAL COLLEGE

NAPERVILLE, ILLINOIS
FEBRUARY 19, 1941

Published every Tuesday during the Collegiate Year

SUBSCRIPTION $2.25 Per Year

Practical Punsters Perpetrated Pranks!

By Mary Arlen

Practical jokers will be practical jokers and North Central has always had them. For instance, the students used to put an alarm clock in the organ in Koten chapel, setting it so that it would go off at a particular time. During the sermon? My! My!

Then there was the time somebody draped the zoology's dreadfully live looking skeleton over the top of the organ pipes in chapel. Imagine what the students thought when they saw that confronting them as they entered! Prof Pinney never let on, until chapel was over and he announced, "Will the pranksters please take the skeleton down."

Probably more than one person has often wondered who did the deed. Boys will be boys!

THE COLLEGE CHRONICLE OF NORTH CENTRAL COLLEGE
NAPERVILLE, ILLINOIS
WEDNESDAY, OCTOBER 5, 1949

Oscar II Begins His Athletic Career!

Timidly this reporter ventured out upon the athletic field. Dodging a flying tackle and stepping daintily over a pile of struggling football players, she approached Coach Simmons to ask, "Tell me about the athletic department's new addition, Coach."

Coach Simmons looked down at the reporter and smiled, "We have a lovely new member in our athletic department, Oscar the Second."

"He or she, Coach?"

"We can't tell for sure. If it's a man, he was short. If it's a woman, she was tall."

"Stop, Coach. I'm confused. What does this mean? Why can't you tell for sure?"

Coach Simmons continued happily, "This Oscar cost North Central a lot of money. Yes, sir, $335.00. And he's perfect, has all his parts!"

"How do you spell that last name, Coach?" asked our befuddled reporter.

"Oscar the Second is a replacement for Oscar! Original Oscar's skeleton came from the first man hanged right here in DuPage County."

"Skeleton? You mean the man's bones?"

"Of course. The first Oscar put in many years of hard service in Zoology classes here. He endured many indignities such as being used in countless 'Tunnels of Horror' in our fieldhouse, and suffered accidents which broke his right clavicle, right scapula, and his pelvic bone."

"How terrible!"

"Yes, would you believe it, the first Oscar also had a cracked skull, broken phalanges, a broken breastbone, floating ribs, and was missing one leg."

"No!"

"So naturally we had to retire him! But we're very happy with our new Oscar. He's more than complete, because on his right side he has in red and blue all the origins and insertions of muscles and ligaments. He has his own closet. We're going to protect our lovely new skeleton, I can tell you!"

"And what will become of the retired one-legged Oscar the First?"

"Our Biology department is keeping his teeth and I'll give his bones a nice closet to rest in. He is a Naperville legacy after all!"

"The Tunnels of Horror," Amir said. He shook his head and thought of the multitude of ways Patrick Doyle had been mistreated in death. Everything was making sense, including the chapel music he and Ravi had both heard.

Vejin reached under her desk for the printer, retrieved the printed articles, and handed them to Amir. "Do you think the Biology Department might have the teeth?" Amir asked.

"Perhaps? Ali can hunt for them with her access to the science labs. I don't want to squash your hopes, but since 1949, that building has been renovated at least once. I very much doubt we still have the skeleton, but there is no record of it being *destroyed,* either."

Sabiha pointed to the computer screen and said, "Maybe Coach Simmons kept it at home."

"Let me look him up," Vejin said, typing on her keyboard. The three looked from her screen to the open door of Vejin's office as Ali entered.

"Any luck?" Ali said. Her cheeks were flushed as though she'd been running.

"We're hoping you can locate his teeth," Amir said and handed her the printed copies. "Last documented in 1949."

"I'll keep looking for the last man to know the whereabouts of his skeleton," Vejin said. "Who was Coach Simmons?" She said aloud to her computer.

CHAPTER THIRTY

———— ·•✦•✦•✦•· ————

R enée's driver, a man in a brown suit and a cap, was standing outside the car. He came over to assist Camille with her baggage. "Good morning and welcome," he said, tipping his hat. "I've been told you are fluent in French, which is good because I don't know any other language."

Sami was deep asleep in her stroller seat, which doubled as a car seat, and Camille lifted it into the passenger rear side. Once they were all buckled in, her mother sat with them in the back, the driver proceeded along A1. Traffic was light, and as the sun was rising, they passed the IKEA store. "Monstrous," her mother said, with a tilt of her head to the iconic blue and yellow warehouse.

The drive sparked memories of her childhood, and her father. She remembered his distaste for McDonalds' arrival in France. He'd taken her after she pleaded, and watched as she and Viva tasted their first French fries. "French," he'd said, "nothing about these potatoes are French." He laughed despite himself when he tasted one. "Oh, those are good, though, aren't they?"

Camille was surprised by the anti-government graffiti along the highway's concrete walls.

"Yellow Vesters," Renée said. "They're ruining our country. With each protest, every day. They burn cars and tear down barriers all while waving the French flag."

"They're fed up with the rising prices and cost of living," Camille explained. "They feel like the political elite has forgotten them."

"So they burn our country? These so-called patriots?"

Camille noticed their driver's eyes in the rearview mirror as his gaze studied her before returning to the road. "They pay high taxes with little in return," Camille said.

Renée waved her hand, with a quick dismiss of the topic. "Immigrants. We should never have allowed so many in. You say raise taxes on gasoline, and they say strike."

Camille shook her head. Some things never changed. It was a battle she'd fought and lost too many times to count. Sami stirred, opening her eyes to find her mother before closing them again. Her chest rose and fell as she drifted back to sleep.

They traveled through the roundabout intersection at the Arc de Triomphe, and Camille noticed the metal police barricades. Assuming it was due to the protests, she didn't mention it. The streets became narrow and tree-lined with cobblestones and sidewalks. They were nearing her mother's home, a hidden oasis with a courtyard and private heated pool, on Rue Laromiguière, two blocks away from cafés and nightlife. She imagined what the "Yellow Vesters" would think of it.

The driver parked in front of the freshly painted wood doors, now the color of forest green. She preferred their former burgundy but didn't say so. She carried Sami inside, leaving the seat latched in place, and the driver brought her things inside.

The interior appeared unchanged and felt more like a museum than a home, with its immaculate cream-colored walls and floor-to-skylight customized windows allowing a panoramic view of the garden and pool. It had a chef's kitchen for staff to prepare elaborate meals for dignitaries and friends; Renée routinely hosted fundraisers and parties, considering herself a philanthropist of the arts. She displayed elegant abstract pieces, only from French artists, along the walls of her home, and each one had custom lighting. There were no family photos downstairs.

Camille examined a piece by an artist she hadn't seen before. It was a framed acrylic on canvas, an abstract of her mother's garden.

"I had that one commissioned; Philippe Abril is the artist. Isn't it magnificent?"

Camille nodded.

"Perhaps I'll go to my room for a bit, *Maman,* and nap with Sami."

"I'll rest too; it's early. I had the maid lay out towels for you as well if you feel like showering."

Camille carried Sami and followed the driver upstairs as he took the luggage for her. The sun's early light illuminated their path. Alone in her childhood room, she picked up the picture of her father from the bedside table. Her finger traced the familiar gray beard and kind eyes; he was smiling, holding her and Viva in his lap. Camille was surprised Renée hadn't moved it. She changed Sami into her pajamas and tucked her underneath the covers. She undressed and curled in the same bed next to her daughter to sleep.

CHAPTER THIRTY-ONE

---- ·· ◆ ·· ----

*A*li walked with them for three blocks to the sprawling Wentz Science Center on Loomis Street. The wind had picked up, and Amir regretted not driving them. All this walking was hard for Sabiha. She hadn't gotten her daily afternoon nap, her "*nooach*," as she called it.

"Is this building the Biology Department?" Amir said, glancing at the new construction. It took an entire block in length.

"I wish," Ali said. "It's for Bio, Chemistry, Physics, Psychology, and Computer Science. It's the cornerstone of the 'A Brilliant Future Campaign.'" She pointed to one of the signs for the campaign. They passed the "Golden Ratio Wall," a crystal blue design spanning two flights, the image of a conch shell comprised of two thousand pictures of North Central College history.

"No pictures of Oscar, huh?" Amir said looking at the artwork.

"They probably don't want to share that nugget of history with fundraisers. Let's go to the basement," Ali said and led them to the elevator. "They keep all sorts of oddities in a storage room I know."

They walked the long sterile corridor of the basement, passing a computer work lab and a lounge, the co-eds oblivious to them. Amir thought this generation would never look up from a screen.

"You okay, Savtah?" Sabiha's walker clanged against the porcelain floors. Amir thought she looked tired. "You can wait in the lounge if you want to rest a bit."

She waved her hand, "I'm fine, *motek*."

Ali swiped her badge to unlock a room, one which housekeeping apparently didn't have access to, Amir thought, from the musty smell. Ali flicked the light switch, and the fluorescent bulbs illuminated from above. Dust covered the multitude of shelves.

"Most of this stuff's broken," Ali said, pointing to rows of outdated lab equipment. "It's surprising they transferred this garbage to the new facilities, but here we are." She waved her arm in front of her like a gameshow host displaying their prizes. "The room where science refuses to die."

Sabiha found a chair and sat, her gaze upon the nearby shelves, and Ali and Amir walked further inside. "I'll take this section if you want to look over there," Ali pointed to the back of the room.

Amir did as suggested. He saw boxes labeled Bunsen burners, flasks, measuring cups, as well as more oversized items like a centrifuge and incubator—nothing tagged "dental" or "Doyle." He kept searching, using the flashlight from his smartphone.

After an hour, he looked at Sabiha; she'd fallen asleep seated by her walker with her head cradled in her arms. He needed to get her home. He was about to say something when he heard Ali whistle.

"Look what's hiding in the basement of the ivory tower," Ali said. He found her pointing to a box out of her reach on the highest shelf. Amir followed her gaze and spotted a worn cardboard box, the size of a large coffee mug, with writing in black faded marker. "I believe that says *Oscar*!"

"Savtah!" Amir called out. "Ali may have found it." He couldn't reach it either, so he vaulted onto the top of the counter.

"Be careful," Sabiha said and walked toward them.

Amir reached for the box on the top shelf, opened it, and gasped. Inside was a human jaw with a complete set of teeth. A white label on the maxillary bone read *Patrick Doyle* in bold type. He handed the box to Ali and hopped down.

"It's him?" Sabiha said.

"Appears so," Ali said and lifted the teeth out of the box. "Looks like a full set. He had a space between his two front teeth, you see? Like Madonna."

"Can we just take it?" Sabiha said.

"He's been here for over a hundred and sixty years," Ali said. "Better to ask forgiveness than permission."

"So, once we find his skeleton, we'll have the DNA from this to match it to him," Amir said and texted Camille.

We found Doyle's teeth. We're closing in.

She responded within seconds.

Hurry. I want to come home, missing you terribly.

He texted back, a smile on his lips.

Soon. Very soon.

···✦✦✦✦···

It was nightfall and the temperature had dropped ten degrees as they were leaving the Science Center. As they walked down the handicapped ramp, Ali got a text. "Vejin has more information," she said, looking at her phone. "She says to come to the library. I need to get back to Ravi. Amir, you'll keep the teeth? Keep me posted?"

"Thank you, Ali. We never would've found this without you." Amir grasped the box. "I'm going to run to the car and pick you up, Savtah."

Amir jogged to the Tesla. He wrapped Doyle's teeth in one of Sami's jackets and put them in the front trunk. Doyle liked Sami, so Amir hoped he'd understand the connection and not terrorize her while the hunt for the remains continued.

He picked up Sabiha and dropped her at the library entrance before parking again. Vejin was waiting for them, excited to share her findings.

"I found the coach," Vejin said, while ushering Amir and Sabiha into her office. "Once I located his full name it was easy. He was a football legend, there's a lot of information on him."

She handed him a printout from Wikipedia. "Guernsey Elmor Simmons," Vejin said. "Looks like he was a handsome all-star in his time, and was even inducted into the National Association of Intercollegiate Athletics Hall of

Fame. He coached track and football at North Central for twenty years, and passed from a sudden heart attack at the age of sixty-five."

"Any offspring?" Amir said.

"One son, deceased. Three grandchildren and six great-grandchildren, one of whom is a local physician, actually," Vejin said with a glance to Amir. "Stephen Simmons, MD. Know him?"

"His name's familiar. I think he's on staff at the hospital."

"He's a pediatrician; he looks like his great-grandfather with those deep-set eyes and powerful chin. Impressive lineage," Vejin said, pointing to the two images she cut and pasted onto her screen; one picture was the coach in black and white from 1940, the other in color of Stephen Simmons. "He lives right down the street in one of the old Victorian era houses. I suspect it's a family home passed through generations, because there are no recent bills of sale or property records for it."

Amir and Sabiha thanked Vejin and went back outside.

"What if he lives in his great-grandfather's home?" Sabiha said. "We should just go and ask."

"He'll think we're crazy," Amir said.

"Not if he's being haunted, too. He'll be desperate to help."

CHAPTER THIRTY-TWO

————— ·•◆•· —————

The Simmons home was less than half a mile away on Sleight Street, in the historic residential downtown district. Looking at the house, Amir figured it was likely over four thousand square feet with an attic and basement. The wrap porch balcony looked recently renovated, as did the shingled roof and picket fence. The siding was original, with fresh grayish-purple paint and white shutters. Signs for two local teams, North Lacrosse and NNHS Basketball, both Naperville North High School teams, were displayed in the grass by the front porch steps.

Amir took a deep breath and said "Let's do this," and helped Sabiha out of the car. They walked to the front door; Sabiha stayed on level ground, and Amir took the porch steps, rang the bell, then stepped back down to stand with Sabiha.

A lanky teenage girl with her hair in pigtails opened the door, and peered at them through the storm door, a look of confusion on her face as she studied the two. She flipped on the porch lights, pushed the storm door slightly ajar and said, "Yes?"

"Sorry to bother you, my dear," Sabiha said. She patted Amir's arm. "My grandson here works with your father, Dr. Simmons. Could you tell him Dr. Hadad is outside and needs to speak with him urgently?"

"Sure." The girl shut the door. Less than a minute later, Dr. Stephen Simmons came outside. Amir recognized him from the physician dining room; they often crossed paths but never interacted since Amir didn't do any pediatric cases. Stephen extended his hand to Amir. "Dr. Hadad, nice to see you."

"It's Amir," he said and introduced Sabiha, followed with an apology for the unannounced visit. "We have some information we'd like to share with you; it's a sensitive topic that involves your family. I didn't think it was appropriate to discuss at work."

"Well, come inside. Please." Stephen held the storm door open and beckoned them in. He led them to the parlor, an elegant room with deep blue walls, a baby grand piano, and a Monet above the fireplace. "Would you like something to drink? Tea?"

"Yes," Sabiha said. "Your home's beautiful; this mahogany table is so elegant."

"Thank you. I restored that table in my shed; it's a pastime of mine," Stephen said. "The house has been in our family since construction in 1942. I try to maintain it."

When Stephen left the room, Sabiha shot Amir a look and whispered, "1942. Doyle could be here." Amir held the newspaper clippings in the folder Vejin had given him, tapping his foot with nervous energy. He could feel Doyle's presence as an unsettling tingling in his back, as if the spirit was behind him. He hoped it wouldn't speak.

When Stephen returned, he held two cups of tea. "It's cold in here," he said, placing the cups on coasters on the mahogany coffee table. "Let me turn the heat up." He fiddled with the wall thermostat and took a seat across from them. "What's on your mind, Amir?"

Amir took a deep breath. "Did this home belong to your great-grandfather back in 1949?" Amir looked at the papers in his lap. "Guernsey Elmor Simmons?"

"Actually, yes. It was my parents' until recently, I grew up here with my sisters. My wife, she's at a piano recital with our youngest or I'd introduce you. We bought it from my parents two years ago, and they moved to a condo."

"Have you ever experienced anything odd here?" Amir said.

"Odd, how?" Stephen said.

"Voices, electrical malfunctioning, black smoke? Organ music?"

Stephen stood. "What?" He paced in front of them and rubbed a hand through his thick hair. "How would you know that?" he whispered.

"Because I've experienced it too. I know this sounds crazy but we believe it's a ghost, and he wants us to bury him. He's killing my patients; we must stop him." Amir handed Stephen the news clippings. "Please, sit. Read these and I will explain everything."

Stephen took the folder and sat. He read it, flipping from page to page. His hands were shaking when he handed it back.

"1949," Amir said. "That's the last article we have. Your great-grandfather said he would find Oscar 'a closet to rest in.' We've found the teeth, now we need to find the skeleton."

"You think I have it?" Stephen said. "I don't have any idea where it could be!"

"Dr. Simmons," Sabiha said. "Of course you don't. We believe he hid it somewhere here. Maybe your parents, or siblings, might know?"

"Human remains from 1854. Here?" Stephen repeated. "In the house?"

"You've experienced the ghost?" Sabiha said. "Doesn't it make sense it is here?"

"I've never experienced what you describe. A ghost killing my patients."

"Steve," Amir said.

"I'd like you to go." Stephen extended his hand to the door. "Please."

Amir and Sabiha stood. Amir reached into his wallet and handed Stephen his business card. "My cell's on the back, please call when you feel ready to talk about this. Doyle deserves to rest, and he won't leave you, or us, alone until he can."

CHAPTER THIRTY-THREE

⋯•◆•⋯

Stephen Simmons couldn't sleep. He looked at Lillian resting next to him. She slept lightly most nights, suffering from back pain, and he didn't want to disturb her. The bedside clock read 2:23. He stared at the ceiling, thinking of the news clippings Amir and Sabiha showed him earlier that evening. Seventy years ago, his great-grandfather had joked about the remains of an executed man. Would he have hidden the skeleton in his own home? Was it still here?

There had been those occurrences Amir referred to—the black, damp smoke and electrical outages. At each instance, Stephen had reasoned it away, assuming it was his imagination. Most recently, their smart home device, Alexa, would randomly play church organ music with no prompting or commands and it would take multiple attempts to turn it off. He and Lillian thought it was an electrical glitch, while the kids joked Alexa was possessed.

Stephen didn't believe in ghosts. All those years ago, his mother had said to never speak of their strange experience, and he hadn't. Even if everything written was true, and his great-grandfather had kept the skeleton, so what? He probably threw it away. He turned to his side and wrapped his arm over his wife; she curled against him. He wasn't going to burden her with this nonsense. As he drifted to sleep, a tremendous bang, the sound of glass shattering, jolted him and Lillian awake.

"What was that?" Lillian said, upright.

"Don't move," Stephen whispered. He flipped the bedside lamp on and pointed to the terrace glass door. It was spiderwebbed with cracks as if struck with a tremendous force. He put on his bedroom slippers and walked closer.

There was no sign of any projectile mass, only the cracked window. He turned the patio light on and looked into the vacant backyard garden. Their smart home device played church organ music.

"Lily?" Stephen's voice a whisper. He looked at his wife, who was sitting in bed, grasping the duvet to her chest. "We have a ghost. His name is Doyle."

· · ◆ ◆ ◆ ◆ · ·

Stephen, carrying his son's lacrosse stick, and Lillian, wielding a kitchen knife, proceeded through the house. The house alarm was undisturbed and there was nothing amiss on the security camera footage. No one had been in their backyard all evening. They went upstairs to check on the kids; all three were sleeping undisturbed as only teenagers could.

Stephen made a pot of coffee and sat with Lillian in the kitchen nook. He explained all that occurred with Amir and Sabiha, and as Lillian listened, her fearful expression changed to surprise as her pupils dilated and her mouth dropped open.

"They think the skeleton's here?" She looked around the kitchen, and her gaze fell upon the door leading to the basement. She patted her bangs out of her eyes as she did when the blonde strands had grown too long. "We would know if it was buried here, for Christ's sake. I know every inch of this house. You grew up here! You would've seen it."

"I may have seen him."

"What? You may have seen whom? Now?" She picked the knife up and looked around. "Do you see him now?"

"When I was a kid." Stephen took the knife from her and set it on the table. He held her petite hand in his. "My mom was preparing dinner and this black smoke appeared before us. It was like a shadow of a cloaked man. Maybe it was there for five seconds before it vanished. She was so freaked out, we left the house and went to Arby's for dinner."

Lillian took a deep breath and exhaled slowly as she looked at their vacant kitchen. "A cloaked man was in our kitchen."

"Forty or so years ago, yes."

Lillian bit her nails.

"We could ask my mom about it," Stephen said.

"And drag her into this nightmare? No."

"So, what should we do?"

"We're getting out of here and we're going a lot further than Arby's." Lillian went to the bedroom adjacent to the kitchen and pointed to a large suitcase in the walk-in closet. Stephen lifted it from the closet shelf and placed it on the bench at the foot of the bed. "Call Amir; it's his ghost. He can find it," Lillian said and unzipped the suitcase.

CHAPTER THIRTY-FOUR

· · ◆ ◆ · ·

The cathedral bells woke Camille, and she panicked when she realized Sami was not still in bed with her. "Sami?" She looked under the bed, terrified. She put on her robe and went down the stairs calling for her daughter.

"Sami?" She spotted her with Renée in the kitchen.

"She was awake when I checked on you; she recognized her *grand-mère* from our FaceTime chats, right, sweet baby?" Renée said, feeding Sami a banana while she sat on her lap at the table. "Our beautiful Samira was hungry." The way Renée pronounced *Samira* was without affection, Camille noted. Despite Amir's Iraqi heritage, her mother had been opposed to the Arabic name and preferred they'd given her a French one. Sami looked happy, Camille thought, maybe because she didn't speak French and Renée couldn't harass her too much.

"Mommy!" Sami extended her arms for a hug. "You were tired, Mommy."

Camille leaned forward, kissed Sami's cheek, and then her mother's. "Thanks for letting me rest, you two."

"Now, are you going to tell me? Why the sudden flight to France?" Renée said in French.

"It's complicated, Mother." Camille poured herself a cup of coffee. "Amir needed to do research and felt it was better if Sami and I took a vacation and let him work a bit."

Renée's gaze followed Camille as she sat across the table from her. "Amir isn't a research doctor, he's a clinician."

Camille peeled a banana and kept her head down. "He's chairman now, it requires research."

"You aren't telling me the truth, daughter. I know you."

Camille took a sip of her black coffee, it tasted so much better than what they had back home, bold without bitterness, and looked into her mother's green eyes. "You know me? You think so?"

"What does that mean?"

"Maman, why didn't you come?"

"When?"

"When I lost my womb," Camille said. "You weren't there for me. I needed you."

"What was there to say, darling? These things happen." Renée tapped her feet to bounce Sami. "It was a medical procedure and it saved your life. Honestly, you were so dramatic at the time even Viva said for me to stay away."

Camille knew Viva had advised her mother not to come, not because Camille was overreacting but because she knew Renée would be of no comfort. As she was now, of no consolation. Renée, at age sixty-four, was never going to be a warm, compassionate mother. She saw it clearly as she sat in this immaculate and sterile home. At least she had Viva and Sabiha to rely on for maternal comforting. And herself. She was becoming the mother she always needed.

"Sami? Would you like to visit the park?" Camille said. She would shop, visit museums, and dine with her mother. She could act the role of "cultured daughter," but would flee France the moment Doyle's remains were located. This was the last time she would stay at 4 Rue Laromiguière.

She'd take the bedside photograph of her father with her.

CHAPTER THIRTY-FIVE

···✦···

Ravi was discharged from the hospital early that morning, and like any patient was eager to get into his own bath and bed. The only residual injury was to his arm, but the orthopedic team was confident it would fully heal. As Ali drove, she updated him on the hunt for Doyle.

"It was thrilling to find the teeth, but then Stephen Simmons stopped us dead in our tracks. Not that I blame him," she said. "The whole thing's so spooky. But the skeleton might be there."

"Do you want me to call his office?" Ravi said. His hand throbbed and itched inside the cast. He looked in the glove compartment, retrieved a pencil, and used the eraser end to scratch inside. He knew Stephen well, having received several referrals from his pediatric clinic—parents with chronically ill children requesting therapy.

"If you think it'll help," Ali said, clicking the windshield wipers on. The rain had picked up so she slowed down. "I just don't want to pressure him. Taking the teeth wasn't exactly legal."

···✦✦···

Ali flitted about, getting Ravi settled in. He took a bath with his cast in a plastic bag, and Ali washed his hair for him. He took a pain pill and curled on the couch, and since the kids were at school, he took advantage of the solitude to watch *Breaking Bad*. He vaped medicinal marijuana, knowing Ali would cut him some slack, and listened to voice messages from his office. His surgeons recommended two weeks off but said if he was feeling better, he could return to work sooner.

As the marijuana took effect he sunk further into the couch and thought of Doyle's vengeance. Ravi knew he was lucky to be alive. He used his smartphone to call Stephen's clinic; it was 9 a.m., so he was surprised when the answering service picked up.

"Dr. Simmons had a family emergency and the clinic will be closed until Monday," the woman said.

"I'm Dr. Patel, a colleague. Could you please give me his personal number, this is an emergency as well."

"I can take a message, Doctor. I cannot release his information, I'm sorry."

His mouth was dry as he called out, "Ali?"

Ali came to the den and made a face. "Vape only with the windows open or it will smell like a dispensary in here when the kids come home." She opened the window and cold air filled the room. "I'm heating up your mom's quiche."

"Stephen had a family emergency and closed his clinic," Ravi took his feet off the ottoman. "I can't reach him."

"I'm calling Amir."

· · + ✦ ◆ ✦ + · ·

The Simmons family was at O'Hare by nine o' clock that morning. Stephen cancelled his clinic for the rest of the week and booked flights online, while Lillian packed for the family. They woke the kids with news of a surprise trip to Disney. The girls, eleven and thirteen, were excited but their eldest, Gideon, protested.

"Dad, I can't miss tonight's practice," Gideon said, pushing his jet-black hair out of his eyes. "You guys can leave me here. I'm too old for Mickey Mouse."

"It's non-negotiable, kid," Stephen said. "Hurry and get dressed, Gidi."

"Why're you ruining my life?!" Gidi slammed the door to the bathroom. Stephen waited at the door until he heard Gidi turn on the shower. He wished he could tell him the truth.

They locked the house, leaving the alarm off, and left the key under the potted plant on the front porch. Before they boarded their flight to Orlando, Stephen called Amir.

"Your ghost visited last night by shattering our door. Tear down walls if you need to, just get him out of here. We're leaving town until Sunday night."

"Stephen, I get it. I sent my wife and child to France."

"Be careful with the shattered glass door. I'll have someone come out to fix any new damages next week."

"Sabiha and I will be meticulous," Amir said. "Thank you for allowing this."

"I don't have a choice. Text me if you find it," Stephen said. "I'll be at the 'happiest place on earth' pretending everything's fine."

·· ◆ ◆ ◆ ◆ ◆ ··

As Amir hung up, his phone vibrated with another call. Ali's name was on the screen. "Stephen's office closed due to a family emergency," Ali said.

"Doyle scared him out," Amir said, putting a collar and leash on Charlie. "We have permission to search the house. The Simmons family's hiding out at Disney."

Ali laughed. "That's the smartest plan so far."

"How's Ravi? Can you leave him?"

"He's fine, resting at home. I'll be there in an hour."

"See you at Stephen's house. Bring a flashlight."

Amir looked at Charlie's uneaten food bowl by the laundry room. He added beef broth to the food, but Charlie wasn't interested. The dog had been sleeping alone on Sami's bed, and waiting by the window, watching for the return of the family.

"I miss them too, boy." Amir said, petting him. "They'll be back soon." He'd pack some food for him, take him to daycare, and pick up Sabiha. He was going to find that skeleton. Maybe Doyle would even assist in the search.

CHAPTER THIRTY-SIX

A mir found the key, as instructed, under the plant, unlocked the front door, and helped Sabiha inside. The rain had abated, but the cloudy sky offered little light. Amir flipped on the lights. The kitchen was tidy, there were no dishes in the sink, and the dining table was bare. The house was well-appointed, with new appliances and granite countertops, but the hardwood floors creaked under his weight, hinting at the home's history. Seventy years ago, Coach Guernsey Simmons said he'd "find the skeleton a closet to rest in." But had he? If it wasn't here, there was nowhere else to look.

"Stephen said to make ourselves at home," Amir said and turned the heat up for Sabiha. There was a knock at the front door, and Amir let Ali inside.

"Where should we start?" Ali said, setting her purse on the foyer table.

"Sabiha, you take this floor. Ali, the basement? I'll tackle the upstairs and attic," Amir said.

Amir walked up the first flight of stairs and opened the door for the attic stairwell. The stairs were unfinished and cluttered with empty appliance boxes. He smelled something musty, like rotting wood, unlike the rest of the house. He turned the light on, but it didn't work, so he used his flashlight to climb the stairs. The fiberglass insulation took up the majority of the flooring, and he walked with slow steps over the wooden planks to the far corner of the room, where the steepled ceiling met the wall. He shined the flashlight along the roof and detected a small leak, the likely source of the smell. He took a picture of it with his phone to send to Stephen.

He shone the light on the floor's support beams. The air conditioning system and two water heaters appeared undisturbed on the area with a subfloor. He wondered if the skeleton was under the subfloor, but the wood seemed new, on closer inspection. If bones had been there, someone would've noticed it while laying the planks down.

Something created a rustling sound from the corner of the room, and Amir turned. His heart skipped a beat.

He crouched and shone the light toward the noise. A squirrel stared at him then scurried to a corner, out of sight. He heard Sabiha calling for him and hurried down the stairs.

"Savtah?" Amir said, his voice loud.

"In here," Sabiha yelled from the master bedroom.

Amir found her in the walk-in closet near the shattered bedroom door. She was looking at the ceiling. "There," she said, pointing. "Do you see the color variation?"

Amir shone the flashlight to the area she indicated. The ceiling was painted white, but a spot two feet by two feet looked as though it had been painted twice. The discoloration of the square was subtle. He went to the kitchen and returned with a bar stool. Stepping onto it, he could reach the ceiling. He tapped along the construction, and there was a distinct difference in sound, from a sharp thump to one less dampened, along the square Sabiha had found.

"False ceiling?" Amir said.

"Appears so." Sabiha said. Her gaze was determined. "You need to cut into it."

Amir took a photo and sent it by text to Stephen.

Permission to cut a hole and look here? Amir texted.

Stephen responded a minute later.

We've never noticed that. The key for the front door also unlocks the shed out back if you need tools.

Amir went to the kitchen and found a chef's knife with a sharp blade. He stood on the bar stool in the closet and sliced a two-inch cut into the ceiling. He pulled back the plaster to create a small hole. He inserted the flashlight and saw a support beam. "It's a deep space. Let me look in the shed. I'll need an electric blade to cut into this drywall."

Amir went to the backyard shed. It was extensive and well organized with tools a professional builder would covet. He looked at the hammers, nails, staining paints, and drills until one item, an oscillating tool with a round blade, caught his attention. He plugged it into the wall outlet and confirmed it worked. He found an extension cord, locked the shed, and took both inside.

Ali and Sabiha had moved clothes out of the closet and laid them carefully on the bed. "There's a skeleton in the closet?" Ali said, "I thought that was only an expression."

"We'll find out soon." Amir said, plugging in the drill. "Hand me this, Ali?" He got onto the bar stool and reached for the drill. The noise of a construction site filled the room and he waved Sabiha to step away. He wished he'd grabbed the eye protection as small pieces of dry wall splattered near his face. He cut an opening six inches long and a foot wide then handed the drill to Ali.

"Stand back," he said, and used his fingers to get under the hole he'd created along the ceiling edge and yanked until a larger piece of drywall fell off. He reached inside and felt; his finger traced the contours of what he imagined was a satchel, soft as velvet, with coins inside. He tugged harder and grasped all of it, pulling it through the hole.

"Someone didn't trust banks," he said and peered into the bag. He held up one of the large one cent coins and read the date. "1944. This is worth a lot of money." He handed the bag to Ali while peering into the space with the flashlight.

"There must be fifty vintage coins in here," Ali said examining the bag. "Stephen's in for a pleasant surprise."

"*Motek*, anything else up there?" Sabiha tilted her head to him.

"Hand me the drill, Ali," he said, his hand extended. "I need to make a bigger cut."

Amir sliced more drywall to create a larger hole and when he reached inside this time, his entire arm fit. He moved it to the right and the left, running his fingers along the cold surface until… there. Something rigid. Like Camille's wrist. His hand wrapped around it and as he pulled with all his strength, he heard Doyle.

Found it.

CHAPTER THIRTY-SEVEN

············•·◆·•·············

*A*mir jumped off the barstool, and Sabiha gasped. A one-legged skeleton, with its thorax and skull trapped in the drywall hole, swung above them.

"Oh my God," Ali said, stepping away.

"The poor soul," Sabiha said, shaking her head. "*Mesken*, to be treated with such disrespect."

"Let's get the rest out," Amir said. He stood on the barstool and, with careful maneuvering, eased the body out. All that remained of Doyle's skull was the nasal bridge, eye sockets, and a cracked occipital bone connected to the temporal and parietal bones. The maxilla and mandible that held the teeth were in Amir's trunk.

"Now what?" He said and lay the skeleton on the bedroom floor. Its yellow bone decay a stark contrast to the plush ivory carpeting. "Do we take it to a funeral home?"

"Call the police," Ali said. "They'll need to start a full investigation. No funeral home would accept it. I say don't touch it anymore."

"I agree," Sabiha said. "We need the police."

Using his smartphone, he searched the web for Officer Nichols of the Naperville Precinct and called his line.

"Officer Nichols? It's Amir Hadad. You came to my home for an intruder call?"

"Yes, Doctor, how can I help you?"

"We have a new… complicated situation. I've discovered a human skeleton."

············•·◆·•·············

While they waited for the police, Ali made tea. "I'm going to call Ravi," she said and went to the backyard terrace.

Amir texted Camille.

We found Doyle. Waiting for police.

...

Time to book a flight home!

...

Let me bury Doyle first.

...

No. We are coming home.

Amir couldn't argue with her. Doyle had been on the plane; clearly he could go anywhere they were. Sabiha sat at the writing table in the bedroom corner, and Amir showed her the text messages from Camille.

"They will be fine, Amir. Don't argue with her."

Okay. Amir texted. *I love you.*

Camille texted back an emoji of a woman dancing.

Amir paced the bedroom and called Stephen. "Doyle was in the ceiling."

"Why the hell would anyone put him there?"

"They must've thought it was valuable. We found some old coins hidden with it. It'll pay for your Disney trip and fifty more."

There was a knock at the front door followed by a doorbell. "Cops are here. I'll leave you on speaker?"

Amir held the phone in his palm and opened the door, but it wasn't Officer Nichols before him. "Amir Hadad?" Two uniformed officers he didn't recognize—a balding man with silver hair and a matching beard that framed tobacco-stained teeth, and a petite, youthful woman with clear ebony skin who wore oversized heart-shaped hoop earrings. He saw two police cars and a van marked *Naperville Police Forensic Unit* parked in front of the house.

"I'm Amir. Officers?"

"I'm Detective Keith McNellis with Major Crimes Unit, they call me Mack; this is Investigator LaShae Tucker with Forensics," the man said. "Can you tell us where the remains are?"

"In the bedroom. This is Stephen Simmons's home," Amir said, holding the phone higher. "Not mine."

"That's me," Stephen said from Amir's speakerphone. "I gave him permission to look."

"For human remains?" LaShae said. "Why?"

Sabiha used her walker to get to the front door. "It's a long story. Can I get you some tea?"

The officers exchanged a glance. "And your name?" LaShae said, pulling out a mini notepad from her shirt pocket.

"Sabiha Hadad. I'm Amir's grandmother."

"How about you take us to the remains," Mack said.

Ali came in from the backyard. "Oh good, they're here already."

"Is this a potluck?" Mack said. "Who're you?"

"I'm Ali. Doyle tried to kill my husband."

"Let me explain," Amir said and took them to the bedroom. "We found the skeleton of Patrick Doyle. The only man legally hanged in DuPage County. In 1854."

"He deserves to be identified and properly buried," Sabiha said.

"So his *bhoot* can rest," Ali said. "He's furious; ask my husband."

LaShae and Mack looked at the threesome. "How do you know this?" Mack said.

Sabiha took the newspaper clippings from the writing table and handed them to him. "It's all in here. We followed the clues."

"You realize this could be the remains of anyone," Mack said.

"It's Patrick Doyle. The coroner will make a match. We have his teeth, too." Amir said. "They can identify him with it."

"You have… his *teeth?*" LaShae said.

"I found them," Ali said. "Labeled and everything."

"Where?"

"In a storage room on campus."

"Where are they now?"

"In my car." Amir went toward the front door, but Mack put his hand out. "Dr. Hadad, I'll need you to stay put."

Amir realized with a sickening feeling that Sleight Street was now a crime scene and all of them were suspects.

"I was only getting the teeth for you," he said.

"Let's get all of you to the station. We'll need statements, including from the homeowner," Mack said. "Investigator Tucker and her team will retrieve the teeth from your car and bag the bones."

"Sabiha needs to rest." Amir said.

"I'll get her statement first, okay?"

Sabiha patted Amir's hand. "It'll be alright, *motek*. They have a process to follow."

Stephen Simmons called out from the speakerphone, "I booked the next flight out, arriving at three o'clock, officer. Amir, you guys did good."

"We'll talk with you then," Mack said into the phone. "Right now, all of you seem a bit looney."

The skull, without anyone touching it, rolled over Mack's shoe, causing him to step backward with a sudden jerk. "What the hell?" he said, pulling out his gun and pointing it at the ground. The sound of church organ music filled the room. The lights flickered and the temperature of the room dropped.

"You can't shoot a ghost," Amir said and shivered. "You should believe us."

CHAPTER THIRTY-EIGHT

———— ·•◆•· ————

"I'll get the teeth out of your car," LaShae said. Her dangling earrings moved back and forth when she bent to unplug the smart device to stop the organ music. She looked at Amir. "May I have your key?"

Amir handed her his Tesla key card from his wallet and said, "They're in a box in the front trunk. I wrapped them in my daughter's jacket."

"I've heard about this key," she said, holding the black card at eye-level and studying it. She turned to Mack. "I'll be out front."

"I'll escort you three to the precinct," Mack said and motioned for them to follow him. "This is spooky as hell," he muttered to himself as he led them to the porch.

Neighbors had gathered and watched from across the street where police had them cordoned off. Amir saw a woman with her smartphone recording LaShae as she opened his trunk. A young man, who appeared to be LaShae's assistant, leaned against the forensic van. She waved for him to join her. They took photographs and placed Sami's jacket and the teeth into plastic bags. He carried them to the van.

LaShae jogged to him and handed over the key. "Anything else that might assist the investigation?" she said.

"It's all in the newspaper clippings." He put the key back in his wallet. Amir's phone vibrated as he helped Sabiha down the steps, and he answered Camille's call.

"I spoke to Viva and told her the entire story," Camille said. "We want you to speak with a criminal defense lawyer and not give a statement to the police without one. You might be in trouble for stealing the teeth."

Amir looked at Mack and whispered into the phone. "I was thinking the same thing."

He put the phone in his jeans pocket and waved to Ali, who was getting into her car, to come over by him and Sabiha. He whispered in her ear, and she tilted her head.

"Okay," Ali said. "Can't hurt, right?"

Amir spoke with Mack on the sidewalk.

"Officer, we're not answering any more questions without an attorney present. I want to take Sabiha home."

"You called us, remember? You're panicked all of a sudden?" Mack reminded him of a Pitbull about to bite—his chest out and eyes narrowed. "What're you afraid of?"

"Are we free to leave?" Amir put his hand on Sabiha's back.

"It's your choice to cooperate or not," Mack said. "Don't leave town."

Amir turned to Ali. "We can go."

··· ✦ ✦ ✦ ✦ ···

Mack stubbed his cigar on the brown bricks of the Naperville Police Department offices before walking through the first floor to the shared Crime Units office. He threw his coat over his worn leather chair and sat at his desk positioned in front of the window. The lake was frozen but was beginning to thaw.

As he typed his report—documenting the time Nichols called him and the sequence of events leading to the skeleton—his rookie, Dustin, came in with their lunch. He told him what happened at the Simmons home as Dustin listened, jaw slack.

"Damn, I wish I'd been there," Dustin said. "I saw a ghost when I was little. I wonder if I would have seen this one."

"Don't be an idiot. There's no such thing as ghosts. But I'll tell you something, when that skull rolled over my foot, I damn near pissed myself," Mack said and bit into the grilled cheese sandwich from Everdine's. Bits of bacon stuck to his goatee, and he wiped it with his sleeve.

"You gonna include that in the report?" Dustin grinned and sat at the rookie desk near the doorway to eat his sandwich.

"Yeah. Sure. They'll think I'm as crazy as Hadad."

"Based on the news clippings, it seems like Dr. Hadad and his crew discovered the remains of the only hanged man in DuPage County. Legally hanged, that is."

"We'll let forensics determine that."

The phone on his desk rang. "Mack." He took another bite of the sandwich as he listened. "Got it."

He leaned back in his chair and turned to Dustin. "Tucker gave custody to the medical examiner's forensic scientists. She says it'll need carbon dating and DNA comparison to the teeth."

"They're so backlogged; it's probably six weeks until we can close it." Dustin put the newspaper clippings back on Mack's desk. "Do we still get witness statements?"

"We can have them do it by email, but let them sweat it a while."

Mack finished his report, and as he saved it, his computer went black. "What the hell," he said and jabbed the keyboard with his thick fingers. "Dustin! Use your Millennial skills and fix this damn computer."

Dustin stood over his shoulder and did a hard reset, but the computer screen stayed dark. "Maybe it's a virus," he said.

"Jesus, I'd just finished the whole damn report," Mack said.

"You didn't back it up?" Dustin held the external hard drive cable and hooked it to the USB. "Why do you ever unplug this?"

"So now what? It's gone?" As Mack stared into the blank screen, he heard an electronic voice, like a man speaking through a distorted microphone, from the computer's speaker.

You deputies know what a noose feels like?

Mack felt a tightness around his neck as if someone were behind him, strangling him. He couldn't get air. He stretched his neck, trying to take a breath in, and saw Dustin grasping for breath next to him. Both men were elevated inches in the air as they pulled at an invisible force around their necks.

There was a crashing sound as the ceiling light fixture exploded, and they were dropped to the ground. The hot shattered glass cascaded onto them. Pieces seared into Mack's scalp and Dustin's cheek and the men stumbled from the room, panting and holding their wounds.

"Now who's the idiot!" Dustin screamed with blood dripping from his face.

"Jesus," Mack said, coughing and catching his breath. "What the hell was that?"

"That was a spirit! And evil as hell." Dustin grabbed a napkin off his desk and held it to his cheek. "Now say you don't believe in ghosts, boss. I dare you. For Christ's sake, he's angry."

"I don't know what the hell just happened, but I think we should put that disgusting skeleton in the ground. That's for damn sure."

CHAPTER THIRTY-NINE

· ·◆·◆·◆·◆·· ·

*U*pon Amir's insistence, Sabiha slept in the downstairs guest room the past two nights. Amir didn't want either of them to be alone now that Doyle's remains were discovered. She'd packed all her essentials, including her late mother's Arabic copper coffee pot, her *Cezve*, with its wide-bottomed round design. Drip brew tasted like brown water to Sabiha, and she didn't care for Camille's complicated espresso maker. As the youngest girl in her childhood home, she'd been tasked to make each guest's coffee, prepared to everyone's individual preferences. It was a ritual she cherished. She placed two teaspoons of sugar for Amir with a dash of milk.

They sat at the dining table, each quietly reading sections of the Sunday paper. "Oh no," Sabiha said and handed Amir the Sunday paper, folded to the second page. "Doyle's gaining power now that we've moved him."

"Shit," Amir said.

"Language."

"Sami's in France, Savtah. I can curse for one more day." He set his mug down as he read.

The Daily Herald

Naperville, Illinois

February 24, 2019

Condemned murderer Patrick Doyle, hanged in the spring of 1854 on Naperville's Chicago Avenue where Sunrise Retirement Community now stands, remains DuPage

County's only executed criminal. But local paranormal experts believe he is a restless and angry spirit roaming the streets.

Many Naperville residents may have had encounters with Doyle and not even known it. For years, people's reports of being confronted with a cold, damp, black smoke were attributed, by paranormal investigators, to the "Phantom." But why would a phantom lurk the streets of Naperville?

Paranormal investigator Butch Neumeyer knows. He spoke to us following an eventful meal he shared with a psychic friend at Ted Montana's Restaurant Friday night and gave us a local history lesson not taught in schools.

In the mid-1800s, the restaurant's location, on Jefferson Avenue and South Main Street, housed Dr. Hamilton C. Daniels' drugstore and medical office. Dr. Daniels was a prominent family physician at the time, with such cures for Gonorrhea as "avoid whiskey, women and highly seasoned foods," and take three teaspoons daily of his patent mercury iron tincture—sold at the drugstore.

Dr. Daniels proudly displayed a real human skeleton in the front parlor of the building. The actual bones he'd dissected as a medical student off Mr. Doyle's corpse used to hang where customers now dine on bison nachos and salt and pepper onion rings.

"We were enjoying our meal, and out of nowhere, the psychic starts frantically yelling, 'He's going to kill him!'" Neumeyer said. He watched as a waiter dropped to his knees, holding his hands around his neck. The lights went out, and in the darkness, several customers screamed. When the lights came back on, the waiter was gasping for breath. The psychic, turning to Neumeyer, told him she saw the Phantom. And before he vanished, the Phantom morphed into an image of a hanged man.

I interviewed the waiter, who quit his job immediately, and requested anonymity before agreeing to talk with me. He wants nothing to do with that ghost. He said he will never speak of the event and is grateful to be alive.

Neumeyer told us of Doyle's execution and subsequent grave robbing and believes the Phantom is furious with the local community. Neumeyer says he's "never seen or heard of the Phantom harming anyone... until now, that is. Something has changed."

According to Neumeyer, Naperville's rich history lends itself to many with unfinished business. Whether you believe it or not, Neumeyer invites you to join him on one of his many local tours, where he promises to let you listen to "real ghosts" as they attempt to communicate and show you their favorite haunts. Nonbelievers, he says, will have a change of heart before the night ends. Hopefully, everyone will survive the experience.

"No one's safe," Amir said and set the paper down.

"I wonder if the detectives read this." She petted Charlie, who had slept with her instead of alone on Sami's bed. He was eating his meals, too, now that Sabiha fed him.

"I'll call Mack. He needs to know about this." Amir said, "We shouldn't bring my girls home."

"Doyle loves Sami, don't worry," Sabiha said, though her words and facial expression didn't match.

"He loves her so much he almost crashed her flight to France." Amir fought back his anger. "I'm calling Dr. Warne, too," Amir said. "Maybe she'll grant me a physician courtesy and speed the identification of the remains along."

··✦✦✦✦··

Amir called the hospital operator and, by claiming it was an emergency, was connected to Dr. Warne's cell phone.

"Dr. Warne? I'm sorry to bother you on a Sunday," he said and introduced himself.

"What is it, Amir?"

Amir could tell she was annoyed by the harshness of her pronunciation of "what."

"The skeleton Mack called you about? Any idea if the DNA match can be rushed?"

"That skeleton's over a hundred years old; why are you guys in such a hurry to identify it? It's not like the killer is running rampant."

"The killer isn't, but the ghost is." He explained the situation in detail, despite knowing it sounded absurd. He heard her sigh.

"I'll ask them to process it as soon as possible," Dr. Warne said. She hung up.

Frustrated, he went to his bedroom and shut the door. "Patrick," he said aloud once alone, "We're doing everything we can to bury you. Please don't hurt anyone else."

Amir heard his own breathing, followed by Charlie whimpering to be let into the bedroom. He went back to the kitchen and watched Sabiha. She'd opened the front and garage doors, creating a current of cold air in the house. In her hand was the sea salt from the spice rack. She sprinkled some on the wood floor by the front door and, passing him in the kitchen, poured some near the back door. Charlie gave the floor a lick, and she shooed him away. "Go crate, Charlie." Charlie sat on the couch and watched.

Satisfied, she returned the jar to the spice rack and began preparing their breakfast of salad, labneh cheese, pita bread and a side of scrambled eggs.

"Savtah?" He glanced at the open doors.

"You can close them in a few minutes, *motek*."

Amir did as instructed. If Sabiha wanted him to know what this was about, she would've told him.

He called Ali to see if she'd read the article.

"We should contact the cemetery in the morning," Ali said. "Eventually they'll permit us to bury him. We can be prepared and purchase a plot, at least."

"It's my *bhoot*. I'll pay for it." Amir said.

"I think it's Naperville's *bhoot*," Ali said. "One that may never leave."

CHAPTER FORTY

··· ♦ ···

*D*r. Petra Warne arrived at the hospital early Monday morning, scanned herself into the pathology department on the first floor, and went straight to her office. It appeared no one else was coming in; she remembered her partner was off for the week. She went to their make-shift shared kitchen, which contained a dorm-sized fridge, a sink, one set of cabinets, and a coffee machine, and brewed herself a strong pot of coffee. She ate a stale donut from Friday. There was one unexpected hospital death over the weekend, so she hoped she could catch up on all her paperwork once she finished the autopsy.

On her agenda that day was to call Sloane Michaels, an experienced physical DNA scientist at the Forensic Science Center, and discuss the unidentified skeleton and dental analysis of Patrick Doyle. There were hundreds of cases in line—rape kits, blood from crime scenes, DNA buccal swabs—and she resented Mack, and now Amir, nagging her. They had no idea how busy she was as the only certified forensic pathologist consulting at the center, which received over three thousand requests per year. All the while, she needed to prioritize her hospital responsibilities.

Amir's claim there was a ghost haunting their community was laughable. She was a scientist, and so was he. She was surprised an M.D. could hold such deranged beliefs but kept that to herself. "I'll have them look at it as soon as possible," she'd told him last night.

"Everyone needs an answer, and they need it stat," she muttered to herself, sipping the last of her coffee. In her office, she changed into scrubs, then took the stairs to the basement autopsy lab, and unlocked the door. She found a zipped body bag on the surgical metal table awaiting her, and read the E.R. physician's history and physical. He believed the patient had suffered a massive

MI and had called the time of death forty minutes after initiating CPR. "No return of spontaneous circulation," he'd written. "The family requests an autopsy."

She turned her back to the body bag, and holding her Dictaphone near her mouth, said, "Dictating on Anna Masmus, February 25, 2019."

She heard the sound of the body bag unzip.

She spun around. No one was there, but the bag was now open. "What the hell," she said and slowly walked toward it. Was the zipper broken?

Dr. Warne, you've been warned.

A man's voice. From her Dictaphone.

The metal table with the body bag rolled toward her, and its wheels creaked against the floor. Ice-cold air enveloped her.

Jesus, she thought and ran for the stairs, dropping the Dictaphone, and leaving the door unlocked.

·· ✦ ✦ ✦ ✦ ··

She went to her office and rummaged through her purse for the vape pen. She opened her window, took a drag of nicotine, and exhaled out the window. The vapor had a ghost-like quality she'd never paid attention to before. Get yourself together, she thought. Your overactive imagination is creating this fear.

She picked up her phone. She had to complete that autopsy, but there was no rule she had to do so alone. She dialed her colleague who specialized in surgical pathology.

"Mara, could you assist on an autopsy today?"

"Haven't done one since residency, Petra. But sure," Dr. Mara Beck said. "I have a case in the OR, still awaiting the specimen. I can come after, though. Like ten o'clock?"

"Wear garlic."

"Excuse me?"

"I can't believe I'm saying this." Petra took another hit and said, "There's something bizarre happening in the morgue. But it's probably just the power of suggestion." She told Mara about her conversation with Amir. "He spooked me is all. There's no such thing as ghosts."

"Girl, that's exactly why I specialized in surgical path. No way in hell I'm working with dead bodies and their spirits. Call Gabriela? She studies the occult. Might even have something stronger than garlic."

"Gabby? I'll try her."

Gabriela Martínez, a pathology technician who worked primarily with histology slide preparation and cataloging, sounded thrilled at the offer to assist in an autopsy and even more excited at the mention of a possible ghost. "Be there in thirty minutes," she said. "I need to go to my house to get supplies."

"Supplies?"

"You can't confront ghosts unarmed, Dr. Warne. Some are not friendly."

Petra watched her office door open, by itself.

"Hurry? I don't understand what's happening."

She hung up and closed the door. This time she locked it.

CHAPTER FORTY-ONE

· · ✦ ◆ ✦ · ·

*A*fter driving the boys to school since it was raining, Ali noticed the morning's article about the Koten Chapel from her computer in their shared home office. She read the story aloud to Ravi, who was at his desk, opposite hers.

NORTH CENTRAL COLLEGE LINKED
—A student-run news site—

NAPERVILLE, ILLINOIS
MONDAY, FEBRUARY 25, 2019

PHANTOM SIGHTING!
By Patricia Medlin

Did you know that the skeleton used in the Zoology department for decades was that of the only man to be hanged in DuPage County, Patrick Doyle? Were you also aware he was recently spotted at Ted Montana's?

North Central students believe they also witnessed what is known locally to be the "Phantom"—the ghost of Patrick Doyle. While students, led by our own Pastor Speer Lewis, discussed the Gospel of John last night, several noticed the lights in the Koten Chapel begin to flicker.

"Just as one of the young ladies pointed it out to me, I felt a movement under my feet. The next thing I knew, my chair fell from underneath me," Pastor Lewis said. "But instead of hitting the ground, I levitated!"

While the pastor attempted to stand on his own, several students rushed to help him. One student grabbed his foot and yanked to bring him down to Earth. Others reported hearing the organ play music—though no one was seated at it—and candles, previously unlit, went aflame!

"There was a cold draft in the room, and suddenly a black cloak appeared next to me. Several co-eds screamed and ran from the chapel," Pastor Lewis said. "We decided to conclude bible study early."

Anyone with further details behind this "haunting," don't hesitate to contact this reporter. All tips are anonymous.

"Doyle's on a streak of terror," Ravi said. "Let's go find the man a plot."

"I need to get some work done, first?" Ali said, "Is your arm hurting?"

"I'm okay, took a tramadol."

···✦✦✦✦···

After Ali caught up on work—grading tests, preparing that week's lecture with her assistant on zoom, reviewing her latest journal applications—she drove Ravi toward Edward hospital on South Washington Street. She turned adjacent to the hospital onto the driveway of the Naperville Cemetery. A sign made of historic tombstone granite welcomed guests:

Naperville's Heritage

Naperville Cemetery

Since 1842

At the administrative office, a youthful woman introduced herself as Felicity. "You're interested in purchasing a single in-ground burial plot?" She said and looked out the window. "The rain let up. Would you like to see the grounds?"

They walked a gravel path; the ground showed signs of spring with small patches of grass peeking through the mud and ice. Felicity led them to an unassuming gravestone; on one side read *Wife, Almeda Landon,* on the other *Husband, Capt. Joseph.* Beneath the two names, *Naper. Founders of Naperville.* "Many of the Naper family are here, including their in-laws." She pointed to a much larger stone with *Robert N. Murray,* and *Louisa C. Murray* sketched onto it.

"I wonder how Doyle will like being buried next to his lawyer," Ali whispered to Ravi.

"We have a lot of notables here," Felicity said. "Here's the grave of a prominent Naperville physician, Dr. Hamilton Cyrus Daniels."

"The doctor that dissected him," Ali said, looking at the gravestone. "1820–1897. He was thirty-four years old when they robbed Doyle's grave."

"Excuse me?" Felicity said.

"Our addition might become a popular stop on your historical tour," Ravi said.

"Do tell," she said.

"Ever hear of Patrick Doyle?" Ali said.

"The 'Phantom'?" Felicity blinked her eyes. "I just read about him in the *Herald*! The murderer that was hanged?"

"The one and only," Ali said.

"The plot is for him?"

"We discovered his skeleton and teeth, which are currently being identified," Ali said. "We're waiting for the coroner to release him for burial."

"Well, that's news worthy, indeed. He's a historical figure. Let me show you a plot worthy of his notoriety," Felicity led them along Hillside road. "This is section twelve; it's the newest development but, as you can see, a short walk to the historical sections two and three."

Ali pointed to the plot by a pear tree and bench. "What do you think?" She asked Ravi.

"It's peaceful. He'll rest easy." He held her hand as they walked to Felicity's office to purchase it. Ali kissed him on the cheek as they sat. Almost losing him in the car wreck had renewed her appreciation and love for him. Their therapist told her routinely that Ravi needed more affection, and she'd become eager to give it.

CHAPTER FORTY-TWO

· · ✦ ✦ ✦ · ·

*G*abby, wearing extra small hospital scrubs and carrying a recyclable grocery bag, was in Dr. Warne's office within twenty minutes. "I'm going to transfer this into a spray bottle," she said, handing Dr. Warne a glass bottle filled with black tar-like liquid. Petra read the label.

Poderoso Limpiador

All-purpose Cleaner

LA BOMBA

Removes evil odors, jinxes, curses, and brings fast luck

She turned the bottle and read the ingredient list aloud, "turpentine, creosote, and ammonia."

"The creosote gives it the black color," Gabby said. She poured some into the spray bottle she'd brought. "If the ghost is evil, we'll spray this directly on it. Where do they keep the mop and pail?"

"Janitorial closet. Basement."

Petra led the way to the lab. The body bag remained unzipped, where she'd last seen it. She picked up her Dictaphone and set it on the charger by her workstation. She got the mop and pail from the closet and used the detachable hose under the sink to fill it. Gabriela poured the La Bomba in and used the mop to stir it.

"I don't mind to mop, *doctora,* if you want to start working."

"You're here to participate in an autopsy, not clean." Petra took the mop and cleaned the linoleum floor as meticulously as she dissected, leaving no area uncovered. The smell of ammonia was potent. Gabriela stood guard with the spray bottle, but she seemed disappointed when Doyle didn't make himself known.

"It was my overactive imagination," Petra said and washed her hands. "There's no ghosts, Gabby. Let's begin."

She explained each step of the autopsy and allowed Gabby to use the scalpel to dissect along with her. "You have good hands," Petra said, supervising the slicing of the liver.

Gabby looked at her, confused. "Did you hear that?"

"Hear what?"

"A man. He wants me to stab you!" Gabby's gaze was unwavering as she moved slowly toward Petra.

Petra grabbed the spray bottle off the table. "Gabby, close your eyes!" She said and sprayed the solution in Gabby's face.

Gabby screamed, dropped the scalpel, and ran to sink. Sobbing, she ran cold water over her face.

"I'm so sorry, Gabby! Are you okay? You said to spray it if I saw him, and I think he... he was inside you," Petra fought back her tears. She rubbed Gabby's back, held back her thick raven hair, and helped her wash the black liquid off her face and neck. "Are you okay?"

"He's so angry; I've never felt such rage or such sadness." She dried her face with the paper towel Petra handed her. "He is a tortured soul. Are you okay, Dr. Warne? Did I hurt you?"

"I'm alright. But let's get the hell out of here."

"Vámonos." Gabriela grabbed her purse.

Petra locked the lab, and the two ran upstairs, leaving the unfinished autopsy of Anna Masmus, her body parts in varying degrees of analysis, strewn across the workspace.

Gabby and Petra grabbed their belongings from Petra's office and bolted through the hospital reception area. Standing outside the hospital's front entrance, they put their coats on under the awning to stay dry. The pouring rain had lightened, but the valet team was still busy unloading patients. An older man coughed and an attendant helped him into a wheelchair.

Petra called the office of the CEO. "I need to speak with Dr. Higbee. It's an emergency," she said.

·· • ✦ ✦ • ··

Gabby and Petra drank hot chocolate at the Dunkin Donuts by the hospital. Directly across the street was the Naperville Cemetery. Gabby was texting with her eleven siblings on a group message of WhatsApp. "They have lots of advice," she told Petra. "Anna Mercedes was possessed when she was young."

"Do they believe he'll leave us alone once he's buried?"

"He might? You never know with angry ghosts." Gabby took a sip of her cocoa. "Every spirit that lingers is here for a reason. Take my abuela. She died eight years ago from old age, you know. But my mom sees her all the time. They talk."

"Why? I mean, why is your grandmother still here? As you say."

"She's too bossy, can't let go."

Petra watched as a couple strolled the cemetery grounds; the man's arm was in a cast held by a sling. She recognized him from the hospital, Dr. Ravi Patel. He was soft spoken and polite. She assumed the attractive woman with him was his wife.

Liz Higbee came in, letting in a gust of winter air, and approached their four-top table. Liz placed her iPhone in the flat pocket of her Louis Vuitton tote, set the bag on the extra chair, and sat with them. Petra thought the purse cost more than two months' salary for Gabby; no wonder it got its own chair.

"Hello," Liz said to Gabby, who gave her a weak smile in return.

"This is Gabriela Martínez, one of our pathology technicians. We need to tell you what happened in the basement."

"Why here, Petra? Hospital cafeteria that bad?"

"It isn't safe there."

"Are you alright?" Liz leaned in, her deep voice in a whisper. "What happened?"

"Have you heard of Patrick Doyle?" Petra said. "There was an article about him in Sunday's Herald."

"The ghost at Ted Montana's?" Liz said. "I thought that was a satire piece like they post in *The Onion*."

"Doyle's no joke, Dr. Higbee," Gabby said. "Please don't make fun of him."

"I've been assisting the Major Crimes Unit in identifying human remains," Petra said. "In fact, Amir Hadad, the radiologist? He discovered them."

"Amir?" Liz said.

"He found a skeleton in a false ceiling at Stephen Simmons's home. Doyle has been haunting Stephen and terrorizing Amir. And now, we think Doyle's after us." She pointed to her and Gabby.

"Dr. Stephens, the pediatrician?" Liz rubbed her forehead and looked at the two women across from her. "You believe a ghost is after you?" she said. "In the morgue?"

"Also, there's an unfinished autopsy," Petra said. "Patient Anna Masmus. No one can tend to it, though, because Doyle is down there, like I said. With the body."

"Petra, you're a scientist. So is Amir, so is Gabby, and so am I. Are you telling me you left the body of one of our deceased patients unattended and…" She swallowed. "Unfinished? Because you believe in ghosts?"

"I don't need you to believe me or to judge me, frankly. I only need you to grant me a couple of days to get Doyle's remains identified and buried. Then I'll return to work. The lab's locked. I'll tell the attendants and janitorial staff not to enter either."

"What will you tell the family of the deceased?" Liz said. "The Masmus family? They will be planning a funeral."

"I'll call them and explain the cause of death is pending further study," Petra said. "Fire me if you must, but I'm telling you, no one can be inside the lab until Doyle is in the ground."

"Please don't fire me," Gabby said. "I'll return to the histology lab upstairs."

"I'm not firing anyone. Both of you take paid leave. I'll expect you back at work Thursday morning, Friday at the latest."

"Thank you," Petra said.

"Yes, thank you," Gabby said. "Doctora."

Liz shook her head, gathered her belongings, and walked out.

"She doesn't believe us," Gabby said, biting into a chocolate donut. "But spirits don't like to be ignored."

CHAPTER FORTY-THREE

· ◆ ·

*L*iz returned to her office in the hospital after meeting with Petra and Gabby at Dunkin Donuts. She asked Olivia not to disturb her and locked her door. She turned on her computer, pulled up Amir's urine drug screen results, and read "Not detected" for all substances—benzodiazepines, cocaine, opioids, amphetamines, alcohol, and barbiturates.

So Amir's behavior was due not to drugs but, if she believed Dr. Warne, Gabby, and Dr. Stephens, to a ghost. Liz did *not* believe in ghosts. When you die, you're gone. There is no extracorporeal existence, for crying out loud. How could four of her staff be so irrational? William was dead. So were her parents. They weren't waiting for her in heaven or sending her signs they still loved her. She was alone; anyone who thought otherwise was delusional.

The lights in her office flickered, and her computer shut down. "Damn it," she said. She opened the door, looked at her secretary's screen, and found her scrolling through Instagram. Olivia quickly clicked it away.

"Do you need anything, Dr. Higbee?" Olivia said.

"No system-wide electrical shortages?"

"Not that I know of."

Liz went back to her desk, leaving the door open so she could see if the lights in the entrance flickered. She pressed the start button to reboot her computer, and as she waited for it to load, she felt the room temperature drop. Now what? She was about to check the thermostat when, with a sudden bang, her office door slammed shut. A putrid smell—like a combination of coffee and manure—penetrated her nostrils, and she gagged.

"Olivia?" She called out. "Please leave the door open."

She heard Olivia turn the knob of the door, "It's locked, Dr. Higbee. Are you alright?"

"What in the world? Why did you close it?" Liz said, but as she stood, a force—like a man pushing her shoulders—held her in the seat. Folders and envelopes flew off her desk, scattering paper onto the floor.

A man's voice came from the computer. *Believe them yet?*

She clutched the metal armrests of her chair and screamed, "Olivia! Call security!"

A vice-like grip held her throat as she struggled to get away. She couldn't breathe.

···✦✦✦✦···

She heard the door unlock and the sound of people enter her office. Liz opened her eyes and saw Olivia crouched by her chair, papers strewn on the floor next to her. Had she passed out? Two hospital security guards, a man and a woman in uniform, neither she recognized, were checking the room for an intruder. One opened the private bathroom.

"Dr. Higbee, are you alright?" Olivia said.

"What happened?" Liz asked; her hands were shaking. The putrid smell was gone and the temperature of the room was normal.

"Doctor," Olivia said. "I think we should get you looked at. You passed out."

Olivia rubbed her back while Liz took slow breaths to calm herself. So he *is* real, she thought. And he was after her, too. She felt a wave of remorse in how she treated Amir, Petra, and Gabby.

"I'm okay; really, my sugar must be low."

"I'll bring you orange juice and crackers from the cafeteria," Olivia said. "Don't get up. I'll be right back."

"You can go as well," Liz said to the security officers once Olivia left. "Thank you."

She stood, got her tote off the coat hanger, found her phone in the pocket and texted Petra.

I think Doyle was here.

...

Liz are you alright?

...

Yes. He's terrifying. I'm so sorry.

...

I'll keep you posted on our progress to bury him. Be careful.

She took a moment and closed her eyes. She focused on her breath. If Doyle's spirit was real, and there was such a thing as an afterlife, perhaps one day she would see William and her parents again. The fear she'd experienced subsided as a new emotion emerged. Hope.

CHAPTER FORTY-FOUR

--- ⋅⋅✦✦✦⋅⋅ ---

Camille pushed Sami's stroller through the baggage claim at O'Hare Airport, looking for Amir until she spotted him jogging toward them.

"Look who it is," Camille said, crouching near Sami.

Sami squealed, hopped out of the seat, and ran to him. "Daddy!"

Camille watched as Amir scooped her into his arms and nuzzled her. He spun her around and lifted her in the air. Her heart fluttered as she watched him, almost as if seeing him anew; his broad shoulders and muscular arms; how much he adored their child.

"*Mon amour,* my love," she said as he kissed her. "I have missed you," she whispered.

"And I, you," he said, holding her close.

She looked into his eyes and noticed concern. "What is it?"

"Nothing, everything's fine."

Camille understood it would wait until they could speak in private. "Where is Sabiha?" she said.

"Where is *Charlie?*" Sami said, still in Amir's arms.

"They're waiting at home for you two beautiful girls. How was the connection? We're expecting strong winds here later. We're lucky your flight didn't get cancelled."

"Viva would have been happy if we were stuck in New York with her." Camille extended her arms to Sami. "You want to go potty with me?" The pink bow Renée had placed in Sami's hair before they had left France was still in place, keeping her hair out of her eyes. "You stay sweet and pretty, Sami," Renée had said as she kissed her goodbye. "Like your *mère.*"

"I stay with Daddy." Sami clung to Amir's neck.

"Help him get our baggage, okay?" Camille said and kissed his cheek, and then Sami's. "I will be right back."

Camille walked along the black and white checkered vinyl floor to the ladies' room. While she waited in line for one of the six stalls to become available, she texted with Albert, confirming her presence for Wednesday's afternoon rehearsal.

When she exited the bathroom, she heard Amir calling for Sami. He was walking around the luggage carousel where she'd left him no more than ten minutes prior. Sami's stroller was empty.

"Amir?" She went to him.

"I can't find her!" he said. "I turned away for a split second to grab your bag, and she was gone!"

"She is here. Something probably caught her attention." Camille looked at the passing crowds, wondering what captured her daughter's gaze. She saw weary travelers in coats pushing metal luggage carts—nothing in sight her child would want—but then Starbucks caught her eye. A service dog, a golden retriever, was drinking from a water bowl next to the coffee shop.

"Sami? Sami?" She called out, running to the dog. Her voice louder each time. "Samira!" The dog's owner, a woman in a wheelchair, was startled and asked, "Are you okay?"

"Did you see my daughter? A little girl, just now?"

"No, I'm sorry…"

"She had a pink bow in her hair; she loves dogs."

"May I help you?" A woman in a blue uniform with an airport security badge approached them. Her name tag read "Mary."

"We can't find our daughter," Amir said, having caught up to Camille. "She was just here."

"Okay," Mary said. "Can you describe her?"

"She's two and a half years old, with black hair," Amir said.

"She is wearing a pink bow. And a pink Minnie Mouse T-shirt," Camille said. "Amir, I am going back to the bathroom. She is probably looking for me."

Mary spoke into a walkie-talkie. "We have a Code Adam. Repeat Code Adam." Moments later the overhead speakers echoed her words as Camille headed to the bathroom. "Code Adam, baggage claim terminal three. Code Adam, baggage claim terminal three."

Camille began to run, calling for her daughter. She asked every person she passed, "My daughter, have you seen my daughter? She is wearing a pink bow."

The women in the bathroom joined in her search while bombarding her with questions. "What's she look like?" "What's she wearing?" "What's her name?"

"She couldn't be far, we'll find her." A middle-aged woman with short curly brown hair said, with determination. "I'm Dalia; what's your name, honey?"

They checked each stall and scoured the area, an army of mothers banded together.

But no one had seen Sami.

CHAPTER FORTY-FIVE

· · ◆ ◆ ◆ · ·

"We've notified the Chicago police; officers are en route," Mary said. "Airport security's patrolling the area and reviewing the surveillance footage. Let's gather your belongings. You can come with me."

"Come where? She might be looking for us," Amir said. "She's down here somewhere."

"One of you should come with me to review the surveillance. You'll spot her quicker."

"I'll go," Amir said. He hugged Camille. "We'll find her, babe. We will. She's just wandered off somewhere."

Camille was pale. The army of mothers, now comprised of six women, surrounded her when Amir left.

"Here's what we do," Dalia said. "We divide up and search every corner of this floor. If she's not here, we go down a level. We continue until she's found. Her name's Sami. Pink bow, pink T-shirt. Camille, she might have fallen asleep somewhere. My baby did that to me at a mall when she was Sami's age."

"She did not sleep much on the plane. She *is* exhausted."

"I bet she's just like mine. Having a nice little nap while Mom and Dad freak out." Dalia raised her hands and got the attention of the group. "Meet back here in fifteen minutes, gang. Have them announce on the overhead the good news when you spot our sleeping beauty."

· · ◆ ◆ ◆ · ·

The airport security's surveillance team was in the basement, through two locked corridors Mary accessed by scanning her badge. She stored Amir's luggage and stroller in the corner of a conference room and led him into the control room. Three men were seated in front of monitors; Amir counted ten rows, each row with ten views. Mary introduced Amir as the father of Code Adam.

"Which is baggage claim three?" Mary said.

"This one here," one of the men pointed to the screen at the top left corner.

"Paul, put it on the big screen, and zoom in when you find Amir. Let's rewind to thirty minutes ago, 10:47."

The man did as instructed. Amir watched as Camille offered her arms to Sami to go to the bathroom, and Sami clung to his neck. Camille walked away. He kissed Sami and put her in the stroller, and pushed it closer to the baggage carousel. He turned his back.

They watched Sami looking up and talking to herself. She got out of the stroller and held her hand as if someone was walking with her. She walked through the automatic doors and out of the airport with a smile on her face.

Mary spoke into the walkie-talkie. "Code Adam out of the building. Code Adam is outside of baggage claim terminal three."

Amir felt the room spin.

CHAPTER FORTY-SIX

"Paul, which cameras show outside? Can you follow her?" Mary handed Amir a bottle of water. "Stay calm, Amir. We need you."

Amir took a sip of water. He stood behind Paul, clutched the back of a chair, and watched the video feed.

"These cameras are outside baggage claim three," Paul said and pointed to screens with horizontal lines on a black background. "We have electrical interference."

"Rewind the footage," Mary said. "We need 10:47."

They watched as the feed showed 10:46. Paul pressed a button to fast-forward, and there was Sami outside, alone. She was talking to herself, looking to her side as if an adult were with her. She looked back, as if for her father, and then the video flickered.

A moment later, a black screen with horizontal lines appeared.

"Find the nearest cameras, zoom in, and call me if you spot anything," Mary said. She spoke into the walkie-talkie while she motioned for Amir to follow her out. "Are the police here yet?"

· · · ✦ ✦ ✦ · · ·

Camille checked the nine baggage carousels with Dalia; her heart ached when she spotted a toddler sitting on her father's shoulders near the conveyer belt. Why hadn't Amir carried Sami this way, instead of leaving her unattended in the stroller? Anger brewed and she fought against it. It could have happened to any parent. Her included.

When no one reported any sighting of a girl with a pink bow, she stepped aside and called Viva.

"I'll get there as soon as I can, Camille. Sami needs you to stay calm." Her sister said in French, though she sounded panicked herself. "Have you called Sabiha?"

"No. I cannot scare her like this."

"It's been thirty minutes, you said? Get her involved. She is wise."

Camille did as instructed and called Sabiha.

"I will call the detectives to help," Sabiha said. "We'll find her, Camille. I remember when Amir disappeared at Chuck E. Cheeses. We found him playing with new friends."

Camille heard the announcer on the overhead speakers: "Code Adam out of the building, Code Adam outside terminal three baggage claim."

"They think she is outside!" Camille hung up and ran to the exit. It was cold outside, and the rain was strong. Camille realized Sami hadn't been wearing a coat. They saw police officers and airport security patrolling the area. Police cars cordoned the entrance, requiring passengers to find another route. She saw Amir, panicked with his jaw clenched, running toward her.

"Doyle. He has her," he whispered. She didn't recognize the sound of his voice as he fell into her arms. She'd never heard her husband cry.

CHAPTER FORTY-SEVEN

"You read about Ted Montana's Friday night? Doyle's on a choking spree." Dustin's cheek had a burn mark he kept covered with ointment the emergency room doctor had prescribed. The Naperville Major Crimes Unit was working in the conference room as their office was locked with a note on the front that read:

Do not enter. Wiring unsafe.

Dustin held Sunday's newspaper and showed McNellis.

"Hadad called bright and early yesterday to share the good news with me," Mack said, rubbing his head. The E.R. doctor had prescribed him the same ointment for his scalp burn. "I called Dr. Warne to expedite the analysis. She pretty much told me off. Said I could call 1-800-Autopsy if I didn't think she was efficient."

"You play nice. We need her."

Mack's landline rang. "Mack," he said. As he listened, he rolled his eyes and mouthed the words, Hadad again. As he listened, he sat straighter and grabbed a pen and paper. "What time did she go missing?"

He scribbled the details down and barked into the phone. "My partner and I are coming to get you, Sabiha."

"Hadad's little girl went missing a half-hour ago at O'Hare. Amir texted Sabiha. He thinks Doyle has the kid."

Dustin grabbed his coat and said, "He can attack me all he wants, but I'll die before I let him hurt a kid."

"*Motek,* you did nothing wrong," Camille said and stroked Amir's hair, the wind pushed against them as they rocked, holding each other. "How do you know Doyle has her?"

"We watched her on the video camera, holding an invisible hand and talking. Once she was outside, he caused the cameras to short circuit. He's somehow gained power since we discovered his skeleton; that's what I wanted to tell you earlier."

Mary approached them with a young police officer who resembled the German Shepherd he held on leash: muscular, intimidating, yet with kind eyes. The dog's vest read *POLICE K-9* in bold white lettering and his square head was erect as he sat next to the officer.

"Amir, Camille. This is Ryker with the Chicago Police Department."

"We're going to find your daughter. Do you have any of her clothing, something with her scent we can use?" Ryker motioned to the dog. "Tuco's ready to search."

"Yes, I have her…" She looked through her backpack and pulled out Sami's blanket. "She was just resting on the plane with this." She sniffed the soft fabric, handed it to Ryker and forced herself not to cry. "This smells like her."

They watched Ryker walk Tuco a couple of feet away to the sidewalk curb. Traffic trickled by them, down to one lane, as police searched the area. Ryker crouched, held the blanket for Tuco to sniff, and then said, "*Tsuuk! Tsuuk!*"

Tuco lowered his long muzzle and sniffed the covered sidewalk by the automatic doors. His bushy, tan tail went still and his front paw bent. He pushed his nose further to the ground and pulled Ryker across the street, toward the driver lane pick up.

"He's found her scent," Ryker said.

Camille, Amir, and Mary followed closely behind Ryker as the other police officers assisted their crossing.

CHAPTER FORTY-EIGHT

· · ◆ ◆ ◆ · ·

*A*t the airport terminal's driver pick-up lane, Tuco came to a stop. He crouched into an attack position, his ears pointed back, his muscular legs ready to pounce, and gave a low growl followed by a bark, teeth bared.

"What is it, boy?" Ryker said, and following the dog's gaze, he spotted an orange and white construction barrel, one of many, along the repaved road. Ryker looked back at Camille, Amir, and Mary and said, "Stay there."

Tuco lunged in front of the barrel, biting at the air.

They heard static on the overhead announcements. Then a voice.

If I can't rest, neither can you.

The barrel flung into the air, as if carried by a massive gust of wind, and landed on its side. Where it had stood was Sami—crouched, giggling, and unharmed. "Momma! You finded me!"

"Sami!" As Camille ran toward her daughter, a force—like a punch—shoved against her. She fell back and landed on her tail bone. She stood, furious. "Doyle! Stop it!"

They heard the same voice laughing on the overhead speakers.

Sami began to cry.

"The hell with this," Ryker said as he dropped the leash and ran toward Sami. They watched as his body was lifted in the air and flung into oncoming traffic. A sedan screeched to a halt as Ryker landed on its hood. Tuco's bark was a roar as he leaped at the invisible force while Mary and three police officers ran to help Ryker, who was immobile. There was blood on the windshield, and the driver and passengers were screaming.

"We need a doctor!" Mary screamed.

"Sami, run to me!" Amir said, crouched with his arms open. "He won't hurt you."

Sami looked beside her and said, "Patrick, you are mean!" She stuck her tongue out and ran into Amir's arms.

Camille fell into their embrace and rubbed her daughter's back, kissing her chilled cheeks and head. "It is okay, my baby. We have you," she murmured. "We have you."

Amir kissed them both and handed her to Camille, bundling her in her mother's arms. "Tell Sabiha," he said as he ran to assist Ryker. Tuco ran in front of him.

As Camille rocked her crying child, she said, "Baby, is Patrick still here?"

Sami, eyes tear-stained, lifted her head from her mother's shoulder and looked where she had just fled. "He's gone."

·· ◆ ◆ ◆ ◆ ··

Amir felt Ryker's neck for a carotid pulse, relieved to find a strong one. He saw condensation in the air from Ryker's shallow breath. "I'm a doctor, Ryker. Can you hear me?" Ryker remained still. "Ryker, open your eyes if you can hear me."

"My partner's grabbing the emergency kit," a police officer said while assisting the driver and passengers, a young family, out of the sedan.

"He came out of nowhere!" the mother said. "I was only going ten miles an hour!"

"It's not your fault, Miss," Mary said, leading them away from the scene.

"Ryker, can you open your eyes?" Amir said. He watched as Ryker grimaced, his brow furrowed. Tuco stood on his hindlegs and whimpered by Ryker's nose. When Tuco licked blood off his forehead, Ryker opened his eyes.

"The girl?" Ryker whispered.

"She's fine. We're going to take care of you now. Just hold still. You could have a neck injury."

Amir heard the distant sound of sirens.

CHAPTER FORTY-NINE

· · ◆ ◆ · ·

Within fifteen minutes, one ambulance had taken Ryker to the hospital, and one was administering to Sami. Sami's temperature was slightly low, so the EMTs bundled her in blankets with a heating pad as she rested in her mother's lap. She looked tiny and exhausted, Amir thought, seated by them in the ambulance.

He saw Sabiha get out of a cruiser, with Mack helping her with the walker, and ran to her. She hugged him, and with his assistance, went to Sami and Camille. She couldn't climb the step to get inside to Sami, who was asleep.

"Camille," Sabiha said, leaning in from the street level to touch the stretcher. "Are you two alright?"

"We are okay," Camille said, reaching her hand to Sabiha's and squeezing it. "Just fine."

"Camille was incredible through all of this," Amir said, stepping into the ambulance and sitting on their stretcher. "I fell apart."

"We are a team," she said and kissed him. "You can lean on me, you as well, Sabiha. I will not break." Camille lifted the *sha-sha* from Sami's chest to show Sabiha. "She has not taken it off."

"Will she need to go to the hospital?" Sabiha said.

"It is up to us, they said. I think we go home." Camille said.

"Is home safe?" Amir said. "Maybe we should leave town until we can bury him?"

"It won't matter, Amir. He can go anywhere Sami is." Sabiha said. "What matters is we all stay together. What about Viva?"

"I told her to stay in New York," Camille said. "We should go home, but I agree. We must not separate. Sabiha, will you move in with us?"

"I already have."

Mack and Dustin came to the ambulance and stood next to Sabiha. "Everyone's alright, it seems?" Mack said. "I think the cop's gonna be okay, too."

"What happened to you?" Camille said, pointing to their scars. She touched her head where the two men were injured.

"Your invisible friend visited us a couple of days ago," Mack said. "Mean as hell, he is."

"Language," Sabiha said.

"Sorry, Ma'am."

"What do you mean he visited?" Camille said.

Dustin told her about the computer electrical malfunction, the voice, the choking, and the lights shattering. Camille put her hand to her mouth.

"We're fine, though," Mack said. "Really."

"He wants us to bury him already," Amir said. "Any timeframe? When can we?"

Mack shook his head. "I'm pestering Dr. Warne every day. She's gonna bury *me* if I call again."

CHAPTER FIFTY

······+·+·◆·+·+······

*A*mir carried Sami, who was deeply asleep, into the house while Camille turned off the security alarm. Sabiha let Charlie, whimpering with excitement, out of his crate and he rushed to Amir. Hopping on his hind legs, Charlie tried to lick Sami. "Down, boy," Amir said. "She needs to rest."

"Put her on the sofa," Camille said. "I will bathe with her when she wakes."

Amir lay on the chaise, Sami's head cradled on his chest while Camille curled on the other side of him, resting her head by Sami's. Amir put his arm around Camille and stroked her hair. Charlie sniffed them all and whimpered. He pawed Amir for attention.

"Go do potty," Sabiha said and let Charlie into the backyard. The wind was intense and she had to push against the door to close it. She turned to Camille. "Are you hungry?"

"Just tired."

While the family rested on the couch, Sabiha went to the guest bedroom. She'd returned to her apartment earlier, before the airport terror, to retrieve her supplies. She took the palm-sized sea shell from a bag and added a tablespoon of water to the body of the shell. She placed a white sage incense stick in the water. She pulled a hand bell out of the bag.

She opened the front door and propped it with a chair to keep it from blowing shut. She lit the end of the white sage incense stick, carrying it in the sea shell and shook the bell in the other hand. She walked clockwise through each room of the downstairs, and repeated, "Patrick Doyle, it is time for you to leave this house. You do not belong here."

When she came to the living room, Amir and Camille watched her. She let the incense burn off and set the shell on the coffee table.

"I'll need you to do the upstairs," Sabiha said. "Once you've rested."

"What does this do?" Camille said.

"Earth, wind, water, and fire. All elements are needed to cleanse the home."

"And the bell?" Amir said.

"Raises vibrations." She let Charlie inside. "A standard ghost cleansing, *motek*."

· · ◆ ◆ ◆ ◆ · ·

While Camille and Sami were in the master bathtub, Amir sat on the bed watching with the bathroom door open. Sami was giggling; she stood in the tub and petted Charlie while her mother washed her hair. Amir wasn't letting his family out of sight, and although Sabiha insisted she could "take her *nooach*" by herself, once she was asleep, he'd opened her bedroom door as well.

He called Ali and she put him on speakerphone with Ravi. He told them everything that happened at the airport and how powerful Doyle had become. "We're okay. For now."

"I agree with Sabiha," Ali said. "Moving his remains unleashed his strength. He knows we believe him now."

"Be careful," Ravi said. "Don't be around any patients. We don't want any more victims."

"I'm on extended leave," Amir said. "You?"

"Ditto," Ravi said. "I'm not working until we bury him."

CHAPTER FIFTY-ONE

· ·✦·✦·✦·· ·

Sloane turned on the FMBIO analyzer to allow it to warm up Monday morning. If the center's chief pathologist wanted her help, so be it. The usually calm and utterly relaxed Dr. Warne had sounded spooked.

"It takes up to five days to completely dissolve the bone and release the DNA, Dr. Warne," Sloane explained. "I began Friday; we should wait another forty-eight hours to get the best samples."

"We can't wait until Wednesday," Dr. Warne had said. "Bump everything else."

When she'd arrived to work Friday morning, Sloan had begun the decontamination process of the old skeletal remains by immersing the femur and one tooth in a bleach solution. With precision and experienced movements, Sloane had incubated them in an extraction buffer to dissolve the bone tissue and left it to dissolve over the weekend.

Now, she washed her hands in the prep room, erasing her lingering cat hair, and donned gloves, a bonnet over her ponytail, and a sterile gown. Next, she mixed the bone samples, now a powder, with an organic solvent.

Satisfied with her samples, she placed the first one—the femur's DNA—into an individual well on the plate and labeled the program P. Doyle Bones: 19-0093-01. After she determined there was enough DNA in the sample, she began the amplification. She clicked the setting button and chose the parameters, resolution, and sensitivity and pressed start. She repeated the sequence using a sample of the tooth, labeling the program P. Doyle Dental:19-0093-02.

Ninety minutes passed, and she reviewed the electropherogram images and compared the DNA profiles obtained from the two samples. They were single source profiles that aligned at each STR marker. Perfect. Dr. Warne would be pleased. She called her back.

"Based on the DNA extraction and STR analysis, I can confidently say the teeth belonged to this skeleton," Sloane said.

"If we assume the teeth are labeled correctly from over a hundred and fifty years ago, you've just identified the only legally hanged man in DuPage County's history. Incredible work. Thank you for expediting this."

"What would you like me to do with him?"

"Send me your report; I'll write the burial permit and fax it to you. Time for Doyle to be in the ground."

··· + ✦ + ···

"Mack, I asked a forensic DNA scientist, Dr. Sloane Michaels, for her expertise; we needed a forensic anthropologist, a sub-specialist," Petra said into her office phone. "As I told you, residual Carbon-14 dating isn't an exact science, but it was clear this skeleton was well over a century old."

"Is it him?"

"Based on the DNA analysis Sloan performed, she can say without any doubt the teeth belonged to the skeleton."

"*The* Patrick Doyle."

She heard Mack take a long drag from the cigar she imagined in his mouth.

"Yes. You can take custody from the center. I've signed the burial permit, and sent it to Sloane," she said, rummaging through her purse for her vape pen.

"Amir wants it to go to Beidelman-Kunsch... Says he'll pay for a proper burial at Naperville Cemetery."

"Even better. The funeral home can come take custody, immediately" she said. "Damn thing scared the daylights out of me in the morgue."

"Jesus."

"Nope. Jesus definitely wasn't there."

CHAPTER FIFTY-TWO

- · ◆ ◆ ◆ · ·

"*Y*ou need to exercise with Charlie," Camille said and kissed Amir on his forehead. "We are home and safe, and you will be right back. It will be good for you to jog."

He changed into sweatpants and sneakers, put on his North Face winter coat, leashed Charlie, and put his phone in his pocket. "Call me if anything weird happens. I'll go for a short run."

"Do not worry. Sami, Sabiha, and I will watch a movie together, okay?"

"*Frozen!*" Sami said with a burst of energy.

"*Frozen,* again," Camille said.

The rain and wind had subsided, and Amir did take breaths into a less anxious chest as he increased his speed. He watched a police sedan drive onto his street, and distracted, he didn't stop Charlie from peeing on Limping Liam's mailbox. "No, Charlie," he said, tugging at the leash too late.

The sedan pulled next to him, and Mack, alone in the driver's seat, rolled down the passenger window. "You guys doing okay?" Mack said.

"A bit shook," Amir said, bending to speak with him.

"I have good news. They've identified Patrick Doyle. Dr. Warne approved the burial permit."

"Oh, thank God."

"Beidelman-Kunsch is taking custody as we speak, so you should finalize arrangements with them."

"Thank you, Mack," Amir said. He offered his hand through the window, and Mack shook it.

"Thank Dr. Warne; she made it happen." He gave a quick wave and drove away.

Amir's smile was wide as he jogged up the hill with Charlie.

He found his family cuddled on the couch in the den.

"That was too short of a run, *mon amour*," Camille said.

"They've identified Doyle."

"Really?" Camille stood and ran to him. He hugged her, lifting her off the ground and twirling her. He nuzzled her neck and said, "It's almost over."

Sami tugged at his pant leg and lifted her arms. "Me, daddy! Me up!"

Amir held Camille with one arm and Sami with the other, as he spun them. "You're next Savtah," he said with a wink.

"*Kol Ha Kavod,* good job." She stood, and kissed all three on their cheeks. "He'll leave us alone and rest. One hundred and sixty-five years later. I'll tell Vejin, she's been texting me for updates."

"We can tell everyone. But first, let's finalize the funeral."

·· ◆ ◆ ◆ ◆ ··

Amir called the funeral home on speakerphone, and he and Camille made arrangements for flowers, a Catholic priest, and pallbearers to assist. "Go to our website and please pick out the casket you would like," the kind funeral coordinator said. "Also, please email me anything specific you would like the priest to know about Mr. Doyle."

When they opened the browser for the funeral home, Amir read the home page aloud. "Celebrating one hundred and fifty-eight years serving Naperville and the surrounding communities."

"They've been in business since 1861," Camille said. "Seven years after Doyle died."

Browsing on the funeral home's preferred vendor, they went to the "in stock" tab. He and Camille picked a coffin instead of a casket to respect the burial practice at the time of Doyle's death; it was constructed from pine wood with a white velvet interior and matching pillow. "He'll like it," Amir said. He clicked Buy, satisfied with the purchase.

"Let's call the Patels," Camille said.

Amir spoke into the speakerphone. "Thank you so much for arranging the plot. We have some really good news."

"Don't play," Ali said. "They identified him?"

"Burial permit signed, remains are in custody, and Beidelman-Kunsch says they can bury him tomorrow."

"That's incredible! What time?"

"11:00. Graveside service. We requested a Catholic priest since he was Irish."

"Okay, we'll see you guys there."

They called Petra next, thanked her, and gave her the funeral details as well.

"I'll let Liz know," she said. "He visited her, too."

"Is she okay?"

"She's spooked but fine. See you tomorrow."

One more call, Amir thought.

"Stephen, you're on speakerphone with my wife Camille," he said. "We're burying him."

"Hallelujah, sweet Jesus. Maybe Lillian will sleep, finally."

"I know the feeling well," Camille said. "Please send her my best. And thank you both for letting us search your home."

Amir gave Stephen the details for the funeral.

"We'll be there," Stephen said.

CHAPTER FIFTY-THREE

· · · ◆ ◆ ◆ · · ·

Amir parked the Tesla along the narrow cemetery road, facing the gravesite, and joined Camille, Sami, and Sabiha, where he'd unloaded them. They stood in a semi-circle with Ali and Ravi. Camille had placed Sami in her stroller as Sami was still recovering from jet lag and had fallen asleep in the car. He and Camille had debated leaving Sabiha with Sami at home but were too fearful of separating the family. Also, Sabiha wanted to attend and pay her respects.

The coffin they'd chosen lay atop the metal lowering device, and Astroturf covered the area near the grave. The fog and mist added to the moment's gravity, and Amir looked at the gray-white sky. He wondered what the weather had been like the day they hanged Doyle one mile away.

The priest, wearing a traditional black vestment, approached with a bible and notebook.

"Father Callahan, good to meet you," Amir said. "Thank you for officiating. Did you receive our email?"

"Amir, Camille, yes. I did." He gave a slight bow. "I am honored to be part of this remarkable history."

They waited as the others joined them. Mack, wearing a Cubs baseball cap that covered his scalp injury, walked with the detective Amir met at the airport. "What's his name again?" Amir whispered to Sabiha.

"Dustin," she said. "Nice man."

Amir made introductions as more gathered around the gravesite. Liz Higbee approached Amir and Camille with her head lowered. A silk scarf covered her silver hair. "I hope you both understand about the urine drug screen. I was following hospital protocol."

Camille put her gloved hand over Liz's and said, "Of course. Water under a bridge, as they say, yes?"

Dr. Warne attended with a petite young woman, Gabby, whom she introduced to the group.

Vejin, wearing a black hijab, parked nearby and hurried to join them. Sabiha greeted her with a hug, and they whispered in Arabic while Stephen approached with a blonde woman whom he introduced as his wife, Lillian.

Looking at those congregated, Amir said, "Father, I believe that's everyone."

"Let's begin," Father Callahan said. "In the name of the Father, the Son, and the Holy Spirit," he crossed his hand across his chest and to his forehead. "May the Lord be with you. Brother Patrick has gone to rest; may the Lord now welcome him to the table of God's children in Heaven. Let us assist him with our prayers. Gracious and loving God, send your holy angels to watch over this grave as we bury here the mortal remains of Patrick Doyle. Deliver his soul from every bond of sin so that he may rejoice with you forever."

"We will now hear from Amir." The priest motioned for Amir to stand next to him.

"Thank you for being here and for all your help in locating and identifying Patrick's remains. I've considered what to say for a man executed over a century and a half ago. None of us know what happened; why Patrick Doyle killed a man, or even *if* he killed a man. What we do know for certain is his body was grossly mistreated in death. Every deceased person deserves respect and dignity, but instead, his body was dissected and exploited by the local medical community."

With a tilt of the head, Amir motioned to their hospital, next to the cemetery. "For that, we owe him a debt of gratitude as his skeleton educated students and physicians for over a century. We also owe him an apology, for no person should be preyed upon as he was in death. Please forgive this community for the behavior of its forebears. Mr. Doyle, may you now rest in peace."

"Godspeed," Father Callahan said. "Would any others who like to say a few words for the departed?"

Sabiha raised her hand. "Though we assume he was Catholic, I'd like to add the Jewish prayer for the deceased."

"The Kaddish?" The priest said. "Please." He bowed his head as she recited the prayer in Hebrew.

"Anyone else?" Father Callahan said.

Gabby stepped forward, holding a holy death rosary in her hands, and spoke in Spanish. Camille spoke next in French, followed by Dr. Warne in German, Ali in Hindi, and Vejin in Arabic.

"Beautiful," Father Callahan said. "Anyone else?" When no one answered, he concluded the ceremony. "Ashes to ashes, dust to dust, may the Lord bless Patrick and keep him. May he grant him forgiveness. Eternal rest grant unto him, O Lord, and let perpetual light shine upon him. May the souls of all the faithful departed, through the mercy of God, rest in peace."

"Amen," the group said in unison.

The sun peeked through the clouds, and the fog lifted as the cables lowered the coffin into the concrete burial vault. They watched as the workers laid the lid over the grave.

···✦✦✦✦···

As the crew finished shoveling dirt on top of Doyle's grave, the funeral party dispersed. Camille had invited everyone to their home for lunch, but only Ali and Ravi would be joining since it was a workday.

Amir helped Sabiha into the backseat, and Camille buckled Sami, still sound asleep, into her rear-facing car seat next to Sabiha.

Amir turned the Tesla on and checked the dashboard monitor for any obstruction. Doyle's gravesite was in front of him, and he put the left blinker on along the cemetery side road. As he put the car into drive, Camille grabbed his hand on the steering wheel. "Wait!" she said with her gaze on the monitor. She pointed to the Tesla's screen, warning of a person walking in front of the car. No one was there.

The figure on the screen walked on top of the soil above the grave and raised a hand as if waving. It slowly disappeared, as if sinking—feet, legs, torso, head—into the ground until it was gone.

CHAPTER FIFTY-FOUR

The family, Sabiha included, escorted Camille to Meiley-Swallow Hall at North Central College the next day for rehearsal. The thrust stage theater seated two-hundred and forty, and allowed for intimate musical and theater productions as well as guest speakers. Amir and Camille had attended a jazz concert here last summer. She'd been in the thick of her depression at the time, and watching her now, he marveled at how far they'd come.

Albert and the cast were ecstatic Camille had returned to the role, and no one seemed to mind having her family in the audience. "Do you mind sitting furthest away from the stage in row G, as not to distract the cast?" Albert said. "They aren't quite performance ready."

Amir assisted Sabiha up the steps to the top row, and they sat on red cushioned seats. He held Sami on his lap. Two days ago, Doyle had kidnapped his child. *Kidnapped.* He didn't know how he was ever going to let Sami out of his sight again. Camille, though, had been fearless. She was the mother Sami needed and the woman he'd been lucky to marry. As he watched her with the ensemble cast, she appeared as she had in college, delighted to be on stage, utilizing her talent

"Daddy, when does Mommy sing?"

"Soon, baby, we have to whisper though, okay?"

"I whisper," she said, in her quietest voice, kicking her legs.

"Okay, Brightside, let's take it from scene four," Albert said. "Mrs. Molloy's hat shop. Camille, full choreography, 'Ribbons Down My Back.'"

As Camille and the cast performed, Sami moved to the rhythm. She wriggled off Amir's lap and stomped her feet, as she imitated her mother. At the end of the song, Sami clapped and hopped. The cast looked toward her, and several smiled and laughed. Camille blew her a kiss.

The lights flickered.

Amir scooped Sami into his arms and said, "Sami, is Patrick here?"

"No, Daddy."

"Sometimes lights just flicker, *motek*," Sabiha said, patting his shoulder.

The lights flickered again as Sami reached for her mother, who'd run up the aisle to them. "Patrick not here, do not scare."

Camille hugged her, tears in her eyes. "I am not scared, baby. I am happy you are here, is all."

"You sing good, Mommy!"

Amir hugged them both. "Go rehearse, babe," he said as he took Sami from her. "We got this."

CHAPTER FIFTY-FIVE

········•◆•◆•◆•·········

Naperville Settlement, Illinois
October 16, 1853

Patrick Doyle rummaged through the garbage pit behind Hobson's Tavern, listening to the farmers drink inside as the grist mill ground their corn. The DuPage River was high along the bank, and he could feel the turbines spinning beneath him, powering the mill. Eight months ago, when he first arrived in Naperville, a settlement with only four hundred families and empty fields for miles, he'd asked for a job at the mill. A man's deep-set eyes narrowed as he muttered, "We don't hire no disease-ridden Irishmen," before shutting the door in his face. The streets of America, from New York to Chicago, were not lined with gold for his kind, as he'd wanted desperately to believe—they were lined in horseshit, mud, and snow.

Finding no discarded food, he pillaged the farmers' rickety wooden oxen carts. With the stolen loot secured—three pennies and a dry hat he found in the driver's seat—he trudged through the thick mud along downtown's streets. On Water Street, he passed men smoking pipes and heard the horrid, harsh speech of Germans and the clanging sound of metal pounding metal in Strohecker's blacksmith shop. An hour later, he reached Clow's Dairy Farm. His railroad foreman still hadn't paid him for months of laying steel, but Robert Clow would barter milk for labor and even let him sleep in the barn most nights. Free was better than the "discounted" lodging the rail company offered its men.

After a nod of recognition, Patrick tipped his stolen hat to the elderly gentleman on the front porch. "Thomas's cleaning out the barn. You can go help," Mr. Clow said, his words thick with a Scottish accent. "I'll bring you out some supper if there's anything left to be had."

After spending their Sunday afternoon shoveling cow manure from the barn floor, Clow's ten-year-old son handed him payment: two pints of milk. "What's Ireland like?" Thomas said, watching as Doyle guzzled the milk.

"Green fields like you wouldn't believe," he said, the space between his front teeth creating a soft lisp with the word "fields." "The mountains turn purple when the sun sets. It rains a lot, but we never saw bitter cold like you do here. And summers… *aiyh*, you don't know." His voice full of longing; his homesickness ate him from within.

"So why'd you leave?"

"There's no food. One day the potatoes were clean and good, then the hand of death itself hit the farms. All the potatoes are black and rotten. Year after year." His hand went to his pocket, and he felt the only letter his mother had sent him four months earlier, the words he knew now by heart. *"I cant let you know how we are suffring, but on my too bended neese fresh and fasting I pray to god you may never suffer what we are Suffering At the present… hurry and take us out of this."*

"I came to work and send money to my mother and sister, Johanna. She's even younger than you. Father died. I'm all they have."

"My màthair died in Scotland before we came to New York," the boy said, and kicked the dirt in front of him. His pants held by suspenders. "I was a baby. I don't remember her." He left and returned within minutes. "Sister said I could give you this." The boy handed Patrick a piece of bread laden with churned butter. "I'm sorry about your sick potatoes."

Doyle's lips held a faint upturn. It was rare to feel seen. The famine had severed him from his family and friends and orphaned him alone in this land. Once the boy left, he repurposed the hat as a pillow and used his black wool coat as a blanket. He kept his pocket knife in his hand in case a rattlesnake showed itself and thought of Connaught. He wondered if his mother and Johanna were gazing at the Atlantic, watching for his return.

·· ✦ ✦ ◆ ✦ ✦ ··

The roosters' crowing woke him as daylight came, and Doyle washed his face with water from the horse's trough. He went to the dirt road, passed a barn and caught a ride on an oxen wagon, probably one he'd pilfered the day before. They passed acres of unplowed soil, land he wished he owned.

Arriving on the rail tracks in Warrensville, the smell of a wood fire awakened his appetite. He ate the breakfast, four eggs and hot coffee, the rail line cook prepared on the open flame. He grabbed a shovel and joined his section gang, all recent Irish immigrants like himself.

The Tole brothers, Patrick and James, were cutting and laying the cottonwood planks as he and two other men shoveled in front of them. Doyle's hands were blistered and raw; his gloves had been stolen weeks earlier, he suspected by James. The other men spoke incessantly, mostly about women and Ireland, the two things he missed the most.

"She brings me bread from the house then opens her legs. I'm telling you, softest puss this side of the Atlantic." James spat, then wiped his mouth with the stolen glove. "She doesn't charge me for either!" When he laughed, his rotten teeth were obvious.

As the men labored, the clouds above them grew dark. By mid-morning, the rain became pelting, and the foreman called it a day. "Gather around," he said, motioning to the workers.

The crew gathered under the wood awning, and the foreman, his belly bloated and hanging over his pants, spoke. "Men, we've laid five miles of track this month. The boss man appreciates your hard work." He gestured for James to come to him.

"Sir," James said.

The foreman handed him an envelope stuffed with cash and pointed to Patrick Tole and Doyle. "For you and your brothers. Divide it up."

Doyle stood straight, his gaze on the cash, and said, "I'm not their brother. I'm Patrick Doyle, he's Patrick Tole."

"You look, sound, and smell like 'em," the foreman said with a laugh. "James, that's for you three men. Split it." He lit his pipe and spoke to the others. "Boss says next week I'll have the pay for you four."

James put the cash in his pocketbook. There must've been over sixty dollars from what Doyle saw. Finally, he could send money back home; with twenty dollars, he could purchase fares on the safest vessel available—his mother, and sister would come here. They would farm the New World instead of their doomed homeland. He was their only hope, and he'd made it happen.

James slapped him on his back. "I'd say it's time to celebrate!"

"Let's divide it first." Doyle had no desire to drink with them. He wanted to purchase a warm meal, a clean bed and a soft woman.

"Come on, now, wind your neck in, yeah?" James and his brother walked toward downtown. "Let's get a tall whiskey and warm up. I'll count it at the tavern."

James was bigger and stronger than Doyle, as was his brother. He followed them onto the stagecoach, and they got off at Winfield and Warrensville. They entered the Mens' Parlor of Warren Tavern. As the day progressed and all three men got drunk, the act of dividing the cash remained unattainable. Doyle went through the back room and passed the stabling horses. The rain had stopped, and a house girl was hanging the laundered bedsheets of the upstairs hotel rooms. He went to the privy, and when he returned—the brothers believing he was still in the outhouse—stood out of their sight at the bar and listened to them discuss plans to migrate to California.

"We can afford some land now," James said to his brother. "Can you image us blokes as land owners?"

With great unease, Doyle realized the two could disappear at any moment. The German foreman wouldn't care if he'd gotten his share or not. He needed to get the money, now.

He approached the men. "Are you gonna give me my earns?" His hands flat on the table as he leaned close to James.

"What're you talking about?" James stood from his seat, towering over Doyle. "The foreman pays you, not me."

"You have my money," Doyle said. "Give it to me, and you both can be on your way."

"You thick, boy?" James pushed him in the chest, causing Doyle to fall. "I don't have your money."

Doyle stayed on the dirt floor and watched the Tole brothers leave. He followed them onto the St. Charles and Chicago wagon and hid next to a large woman and her husband. If the Tole brothers knew he was there, they didn't acknowledge it. The streets were thick with mud. As the horse galloped up the hill to gain traction, James Tole, drunk and asleep, fell off the wagon.

"Stop! Whoa!" Patrick Tole hollered. When the wagon came to a halt, he hopped out to help his brother.

It's now, or never, Doyle thought and sprang into action. He jumped out of the wagon, grabbed a fence stake, and beat Patrick Tole in the back. "Stay down," Doyle growled as Patrick tried to rise. He hit him again, this time in the head. Once Patrick was still, Doyle went for the cash in James' coat pocket. He felt the leather pocketbook, yanked it, and began to run. He didn't look back to check on Patrick but heard the other passengers screaming for help.

···❖❖❖···

When he got to Clisby's Barn, he stopped running and caught his breath. His hands were shaking and bloody, and he hoped he hadn't hurt Patrick Tole too severely. He washed the blood off his hands in the horse's trough and asked the house servant for a sandwich. He ate on the porch in silence, finishing the meal with a pint of milk. When he reached in his coat to pay, he felt an empty pocket and a sickening in his stomach. He searched the fabric, tearing it at its seams, hoping it had gotten caught in the material, but the pocketbook must've fallen out as he'd fled.

He ran from the barn without paying and heard the servant call after him. "Doyle! You didn't pay you bastard Irishman. Get back here!"

The night hid him as he retraced his steps to Warren station on his hands and knees in the mud. He felt the ground, praying for a miracle, but the pocketbook was gone, as were the wagon and the Tole brothers. Knowing the law would arrest him for thievery, he paid ten cents to board the Aurora train to Chicago, cursing in a corner with his coat over his head, and wishing he'd never come to this horrid country.

···❖❖❖···

"They robbed me, so I had to rob them back," Doyle pleaded with the Sheriff in front of the judge. They'd arrested him the very next day as he walked on

Randolph Street in downtown Chicago, searching for help wanted signs—the majority read, "Irish need not apply." The Sheriff brought him directly to the newly constructed courthouse in the town square of Naperville.

"I didn't mean to kill no one," Doyle said to the judge. "I just took back what was mine."

The judge, a man of tall stature evident even as he sat behind the bench, spoke to him and the grand jury. "Mr. Doyle, as you have no counsel, I'm assigning Robert Nelson Murray to defend you. His father's Irish, and I'm certain R.N. will do his best by you."

Doyle knew who Murray was; everyone did. He'd been Sheriff Murray once. His father, John Murray, had married Amy Naper, Capt. Joseph Naper's sister, and became local royalty. His family's connections had propelled R.N. to law school, and he'd graduated two years earlier. R.N., dressed for court in a jacket, vest, and necktie, had been seated in the crowd. He stood and approached the judge.

"Your Honor, may we confer with the state's attorneys?"

The judge pulled his gold pocket watch from his vest and called a recess. "Meet back in twenty minutes and not a moment later." He smoothed his mustache with two fingers and stood.

"You'll wait in the basement jail while I talk to the prosecution," Murray whispered to him. "I'll do my best."

The Deputy Sheriff took him to and from the jail as per the judge's orders within twenty minutes. Now he and Murray stood as the judge spoke.

"Patrick Doyle, it's been agreed to allow you to plead at the next term of the circuit court in the spring, so your lawyers have time to mount their case of defense. Until then, you are committed to the courthouse jail. Court dismissed." The judge hit the gavel, and Doyle winced.

"This is good for us, Pat." Murray squeezed his shoulder. "I'll meet with you soon."

"I need to send a letter to my mother." Doyle slumped his shoulders, his hands restrained with rope.

"I'll request permission from the judge."

Doyle was defeated and desperate as Deputy Sheriff Bradley led him back to the basement. "Be grateful you have it to yourself right now. That'll change, sure enough." Bradley untied his ropes and pushed him into the narrow cell, locking the bars behind him. It felt like a dungeon—the only light came from its tiny rectangular window. Standing on his tiptoes, he could see Naperville's Central Park. He watched the winter's first snow begin to fall, and as tears fell down his cheeks, his weeping turned to grunts and painful heaves. He collapsed in the corner, alone. Only sleep brought him peace.

·· ◆ ◆ ◆ ◆ ·· ·

Doyle's pants required suspenders to keep them up, as he'd lost over thirty pounds in the winter months of his imprisonment. His mind lost all focus, and the hunger he felt had abated as his body no longer responded to the need for food. He thought this was how his mother and sister must have felt as they starved alone in Ireland. He'd never received a letter from them and had to assume they'd perished, as he would soon. He had moments of utter rage, spitting and cursing, followed by regret. The isolation, rarely interrupted but for an occasional fellow prisoner or his lawyers, contributed to his declining mental health.

The park's trees were blooming when the Sheriff escorted him out of the cell for the first time since they'd locked him up. The Sheriff guided him upstairs to the courthouse. Local men sat on the wooden benches, filling the room, and some residents stood in the back. A man cursed him as he passed, and the Sheriff told Doyle to sit at the same desk he'd been before in front of the judge. R.N. Murray patted his hand, but Doyle withdrew from the touch.

The trial was but a few hours long, and the opening arguments came on the same morning as the closing arguments. The only witnesses were for the prosecution; James Tole, the wagon driver, and the woman and her husband who'd witnessed the murder. No one was called on Doyle's behalf, as none had agreed to speak for him, including the community elder Robert Clow. "I don't know what this man is capable of," Clow told the legal defense team upon questioning. The German railroad foreman also refused, saying, "...in an Irish fight, you either kill or be killed. Doyle chose to kill."

Murray pleaded for the court's mercy. "Your honor, Doyle… he's but an unfortunate Irish Catholic greenhorn, with pitiable ignorance, who was drunk and desperate for his pay. He had no intention of killing Patrick Tole. He had a knife in his possession, and it makes obvious sense he would have used it if he intended to kill. This was aggravated assault with unfortunate and unintended consequences."

The State's Attorney countered in his closing arguments. "We have scarcely met a man of intelligence since the evidence has all come out, who did not profess to believe in Doyle's guilt. He has committed one of the most terrible crimes on record, and the most terrible punishment which human laws can inflict is his due."

The jury deliberated for less than an hour and returned with the verdict of guilty. The room erupted in applause as the judge banged his gavel for order. The judge asked Doyle to stand.

"The voice of your peers has spoken, Patrick Doyle," the judge said while looking directly at him. "You are sentenced to execution by public hanging. We are a law-abiding county, and we will not tolerate murder on our streets." He hit the gavel again to quiet the cheering crowd. "Order in the court! Sheriff, take the prisoner to his cell. The execution will be one week from tomorrow. The court is dismissed."

· · ✦ ✦ ◆ ✦ ✦ · ·

The day marked for his death arrived. Two local women, Mrs. Rich and her unmarried sister, visited with him as Deputy Amos Graves and Deputy Sheriff Hunt stood guard waiting to escort him to the gallows; the women had prepared baked rabbit pie, stewed tomatoes, and boiled sweet potatoes. Doyle took a few bites but couldn't taste it. He bowed his head as they prayed with him.

"Hail Mary, full of grace, the Lord is with thee. Blessed art thou among women, and blessed is the fruit of thy womb, Jesus. Holy Mary Mother of God, pray for us sinners now and at the hour of our death," Mrs. Rich said.

"Amen," Doyle whispered. "Please forgive me, Mother."

Once the women left, the sheriffs escorted Doyle outdoors for the first time since his arrest six months earlier, flanking him. Floral scents filled the spring air, and the sun shone on his pale, pasty skin. They assisted him onto the wagon and began the one-mile journey to the bottom of the hill at Chicago Avenue, near the quarry. Anger boiled within Doyle as he saw the crowd that had gathered to witness his hanging. The hillside was covered with people. There must have been thousands, even children, celebrating there; vendors offered men whiskey and smoked meats while they awaited his hanging.

The sheriffs walked him along the gravel road through the crowd. One man spat at him and said, "You're gonna die with all your teeth, as you should, you brawling, worthless Irish dirt. To hell with the whole lot of 'ya."

"You're lucky my hands are tied, or I'd whip you to regret," Doyle hissed.

"Now, now," Sheriff Amos said to the spectators. "Leave him be." He guided Doyle to the wooden planks under an oak tree. Doyle shivered when he spotted the noose made of thick rope suspended from an enormous branch above him. The Sheriff put a white shroud over Doyle's body and tied his legs with rope as the crowd chanted, "Hang him high! Hang him high!"

Sheriff Amos quieted the crowd with his hands and spoke with a clear, loud voice. "Patrick Doyle will now suffer the extreme penalty of the law, and the public voice pronounces the execution of the sentence just. Such was the voice of public sentiment, and the prisoner himself acknowledges his doom to be right."

Doyle's arms remained tied behind him, and he felt the hood cover his face. He could peer through the white fabric and, for a final time, prayed to his mother for forgiveness. He felt the noose around his neck and wished again he had never traveled to this god-forsaken country.

He cursed the crowd, wishing death upon each and every one of them, as he felt the planks kicked from underneath him.

He struggled to breathe… until he couldn't.

HISTORICAL NOTES

Irishman Patrick Doyle was hanged in 1854 for the murder of Patrick Tole, and the newspaper clippings from 1854–1941 are verbatim. Doyle's story before the crime is unfortunately not archived, nor are the details of his trial, so the author created his backstory from historical documents of Irish immigrants of the time.

Doyle's skeleton was named "Oscar" and faculty used it to teach North Central students anatomy. In 1955, a North Central alumni newsletter mentioned a zoology skeleton stored at the campus Field House. The university has renovated the building at least once. It's unclear what became of Doyle's skeleton—it could very well exist in a Victorian home in downtown Naperville as the author imagined.

The modern-day newspaper articles are entirely of the author's imagination.

FURTHER READING

Kerby A. Miller's *Emigrants and Exiles: Ireland and the Irish Exodus to North America:* Miller's documentation of homesick exiles inspired Doyle's backstory. The letter Patrick Doyle carries from his mother is a letter by "Mrs. Nolan" (first name unknown), living near Callan, in County Kilkenny, to her son, Patrick, in Rhode Island. It was written in 1850, at the tail end of the Great Famine. Author Kerby A. Miller found the letter, or a copy thereof, in the Public Record Office of Northern Ireland, in Belfast. (No relation to Patrick Doyle).

The Railroaders by the Editors of TIME-LIFE BOOKS with Keith Wheeler: images from the book helped the author describe Doyle's setting and vocation.

ACKNOWLEDGMENTS

I dedicate this book to all the courageous immigrants, especially my parents, Frida Medini and Dr. Jacob Shiloah, who continually inspire and support me.

I thank my publishing team: Copy Editor Ericka McIntyre, who polished the rough manuscript, and Travis Tynan, who proofread it. Amit Dey and James T Egan, my design team, I am so grateful for your incredible skills. Thank you to Keri-Rae Barnum and the entire team at New Shelves Books!

To my early readers and dear friends: Lisa Abell, Rebecca Cox, Heather Huntington, Keren Green, Shira Vickar Fox, Dr. Garry Vickar, Carri Ann Hutchens, Katie Bracey, and Amanda Christopher. You were so generous to give feedback before I sent my second book into the world.

To Dorit Shiloah-Boxer, my Sis, thank you for believing in this book and for always supporting my dreams.

After hearing the paranormal premise of the book, Dr. Joyce Roesler, my best friend from residency, lobbied for Naperville as the locale. Thank you, Joycie, for being an early reader and helping me with the details of Naperville. I am so glad I sat beside you at Northwestern over twenty years ago.

Sometimes when researching a novel, you have incredible luck; my Irish gold came by way of Kevin Frantz, official Ghost Guide and Researcher, who took me on a private tour of Naperville's hauntings and introduced me to Patrick Doyle.

I thank Rebecca Skirvin, Coordinator of Archives and Special Collections At North Central College, and Dr. Andrea Field, research curator at Naper Settlement museum, for the many articles regarding Patrick Doyle and Sean Boers for his legal expertise on police protocol. With their anthropology and forensics expertise, Dr. Krista Latham and Dr. Heather Garvin allowed me to create the character Sloan Michaels—named by readers and friends Dr.

Heather Rogers and Olivia Wilmot. Vejin Abdullah, thank you for educating me on the Kurdish people's rich heritage.

My best friend, Manju Chatani-Gada, happy thirty-one-year friendaversary. Thank you for comforting me when I need it, and celebrating with me whenever we can. The other extraordinary people in my support circle: Paul Boxer, Monty Gada, Dr. Yula Kapetanakos, Dr. Leah Windsor, Mary Beth Darrow, Halle Bennett, Mary Boers, Dr. David Reid, Dr. Judy Ruiz, and my brother Dr. Yoav Shiloah; thank you. My niece Sarah and nephew Jonah, you are my babies too, and I love you.

To my Israeli family, you inspire me with your wisdom, compassion, and love, and I hold you ever close in my heart always.

And to my husband, Matthew Arledge, for understanding the madness of a writer and loving me anyway.

CPSIA information can be obtained
at www.ICGtesting.com
Printed in the USA
LVHW110825080922
726912LV00004B/8/J